PRAISE FOR PAUL THEROUX'S
MY SECRET HISTORY

"Powerful . . . Engagingly intimate . . . Display[s] Mr. Theroux's now patented ability to describe the foreign, the alien, the strange, with both an insider's affection and an outsider's eye for incongruous detail."

The New York Times

"A wonderful book . . . Theroux's gift for painting Third World characters . . . is equal to that of Graham Greene or Somerset Maugham."

Los Angeles Times Book Review

"Consistently entertaining . . . Theroux's hero is a man of ironic intelligence and amusing self-awareness."

Time

"A strikingly vivid picture of a writer . . . Theroux's trademark place descriptions are as vivid as ever, but with MY SECRET HISTORY, he takes us on a journey unlike any other."

The Houston Post

Also by Paul Theroux:

FICTION

WALDO*
FONG AND THE INDIANS*
GIRLS AT PLAY
JUNGLE LOVERS*
SAINT JACK
THE BLACK HOUSE
THE FAMILY ARSENAL
THE CONSUL'S FILE
A CHRISTMAS CARD
PICTURE PALACE
LONDON SNOW
WORLD'S END
THE MOSQUITO COAST
THE LONDON EMBASSY
HALF MOON STREET
O-ZONE*
MY SECRET HISTORY*

CRITICISM

V.S. NAIPAUL

NONFICTION

THE GREAT RAILWAY BAZAAR
THE OLD PATAGONIAN EXPRESS
THE KINGDOM BY THE SEA
SAILING THROUGH CHINA
SUNRISE WITH SEAMONSTERS
THE IMPERIAL WAY
RIDING THE IRON ROOSTER*

*Published by Ivy Books

SINNING WITH ANNIE

and Other Stories

Paul Theroux

IVY BOOKS • NEW YORK

Ivy Books
Published by Ballantine Books
Copyright © 1969, 1970, 1971, 1972 by Paul Theroux

Library of Congress Catalog Card Number: 72-2283

ISBN 0-8041-0517-0

The stories in this collection, except for "Memories of a Curfew," were written in Singapore between 1968 and 1971, though not in the order that they appear here. Some were first published in the following magazines: *Commentary, Encounter, Harper's Bazaar, Malahat Review, North American Review, Playboy,* and *Shenandoah.*

First published by Houghton Mifflin Company. Reprinted by permission of Houghton Mifflin Company.

Manufactured in the United States of America

First Ballantine Books Edition: June 1990

For Anne

Contents

The Prison Diary of Jack Faust   1

A Real Russian Ikon   17

A Political Romance   30

Sinning with Annie   35

A Love Knot   46

What Have You Done to Our Leo?   61

Memories of a Curfew   82

Biographical Notes for Four American Poets   93

Hayseed   108

The South Malaysia Pineapple Growers' Association   116

A Deed without a Name   120

You Make Me Mad   132

Dog Days   139

A Burial at Surabaya   153

THE PRISON DIARY
OF JACK FAUST

▲▲▲▲▲▲▲▲▲▲▲▲▲▲▲▲▲▲▲▲▲▲▲▲▲▲▲▲

SHORTLY AFTER I DISCOVERED AMERICA (THE WORD *DE-fect* suggests error rather than flight to me) it became known that I had in my possession a valuable smuggled manuscript, and I was whisked to New York and interviewed on a number of early-morning and late-night television shows. At some point during every interview I found myself mumbling through my mustache, "Being a member of the Party was for me like being in prison." This awkward simile, intended as a slur on a bungling but well-intentioned organization, was misleading; in fact, I spent all my card-carrying years in real prisons of one sort or another. My convictions, moreover, have always been political. More of this later.

Speaking in a glare of arc lights with the snouts of television cameras sniffing my face, and of course exhausted by what the newspapers correctly described as my ordeal, I tend—I think most people do when speaking off the cuff—to simplify. To simplify is to falsify; I am grateful for this opportunity to set the record straight.

I am frankly tired of being badgered by sneering interviewers about the mistress whom I am suspected of having abandoned, the dozen or so children I am supposed to have fathered, and my so-called "Nazi connections" (I will certainly get to the bottom of this last fabrication and make the inventor pay). Oh, all sorts of lies about my part in the Writers' Union ado over a writer of clearly libelous novels; my mother—rest her soul—has been mentioned as having unkindly informed on my dad; I have been made out to be a perfectly horrible old menace. One interviewer asserted that I received a phone call late one night from our Party Chairman who asked, "What shall we do about Osip?" My alleged reply to this was a silence resulting in Osip's banishment and death. Rubbish! This fantastic concoction is made all the more crazy when one knows, as I do, that our Party Chairman, a superstitious soul, would never touch a telephone: he thought the mouthpiece of the receiver was a source of deadly germs. Another interviewer had the impertinence to ask, "Why was it that you were known as the Mephisto of the Twentieth Plenum?" Spurning the assistance of the translator, I shot back quickly, "Could I help it if I was all things to all men?" smartly putting a stop to *his* nonsense. I am especially sick of these interviewers looking over their clipboards into the camera lens and solemnly prefacing their questions with my full name—something that would only be done in my country in a courtroom or a grade school. Is this intentional ridicule (perhaps my name sounds a bit silly to the American tin ear?) or is it done for the benefit of viewers who have tuned in late and wonder, in their ample distraction, who is the hairy chap on the stool being abused? I know I lost my temper in front of (or so I was told) ten million viewers. There was a simple explanation for that. I had, at that point in the program, reached the conclusion that I was not being interviewed but having my head examined. I have more than compensated the studio for all breakage and all injuries sustained.

On my arrival I graciously consented to the interviews, and now I am terminating them. I have four lawyers working day and night on what I believe are serious breaches of contract; it would be unfair of me to make more work for them by engaging in yet more of these abusive television shows. Editorial innuendo has not escaped my notice either. You are not easy with strangers, you are not above the petty suspicions of your peasant ancestors who left their plows and groped toward these shores as stowaways.

It is not as if I came to this country cap in hand pleading for asylum. Far from it. A narrow-shouldered Italian publisher of Iron Curtain horror stories dogged my heels throughout Europe. He tossed lire my way and, alternately whining and shrugging in the Italianate style, pestered me for a peek at the manuscript I kept photographed on a roll of film in my pocket. Others, French, German and English, each clamored for a hearing. I lunched with each but said no and fled west, leaving in my wake many a crestfallen editor. I am nagged by the thought that my negatives—the ones on my lips, not in my pocket—were a mistake. Both *Stern* and the London Sunday *Observer* offered particularly good terms, and *Paris-match* dumped lashings of francs beside my plate. My accountant is understandably furious and keeps reminding me that on Jersey, in the Channel Islands, I could be living like a king, whereas here in America I am subjected to your spiteful taxes. But let this pass. The early brouhaha here has, after the expensive legal tangle, neither soothed nor enriched me. The bungalow that was so grandly presented to me after my arrival has a leaky roof and a perpetually flooded cellar; and my television is, as you say, on the fritz. Still, I can't complain.

My concern is the diary. It is to this I now turn.

The manuscript that caused so many powerful Europeans to cluster about me is indeed a rare document and deserves patient study. I am happy to report that my present editor has consented to print it in full and has paid a substantial sum for the American rights. This is especially gratifying for, after getting to know you better, I find that you have really no taste for literature at all. Not like my country, where any garbage collector can sing grand opera or quote you whole cantos of the classics. You make a whole literature out of the sordid and silly nuances of Jewish behavior and, ironically, the writing style you most admire sounds like a direct translation from Perplexed Old Teutonic. You love obvious symbols and popular science. Long sentences annoy you, sentiment embarrasses you; you feel safe with alliteration—you think that is a sign of genius. Your heroes are as unlettered as their creators, your gods are all dogs, you have no appreciation of the simple human story.

The following diary if published in my country would be unacceptable and might land the author in jail. But this is not to say that we are an artless people. Other books have readerships in the millions, they go through forty editions in a matter of weeks and have workers banging through the doors of bookshops at all hours. They are read on factory and farm; the authors are mobbed on the pavement, their names are household words, they get proposals of marriage in the morning mail.

Mind you, the present manuscript is an exception. The author is not heroic; he never did a stroke of work in his life. That he is a simple soul is apparent in every craven line he writes. He is not to be emulated, only studied. His story shows just the sort of quaint dilemma expressed in grumbles that is common to a certain sort of person—though no more common, I repeat, no more common in my country than in yours. Frankly speaking, when I left I was under the impression that this was someone only our system chucked up; but since being warmly welcomed in your very lovely country I have noticed that you get these deluded cranks too. And so take this as a cautionary tale: read it to those unkempt sons of yours who stuporously slope along wearing garish beads around their filthy necks; read it to your daughters who lick at drugs and keep condoms in their handbags, and to those uncles of yours who when their god failed began striking out, cursing us with the sorry wrath of the recently reconverted. And those of you who chaffed me about my "convenient departure" and "untrustworthy explanations," remember that although I am hesitant to use this manuscript as a *visa de voyage*, I am aware that it gained me access to your country, and with it in my pocket I know I am welcome anywhere. You need me much more than I need you.

The pseudonymous author of this diary was known to me from youth. As the poet Drunina puts it so skillfully, "We were as twinned lambs that did frisk in the sun, / And bleat one at the other: what we changed / Was innocence for innocence . . ." The difference, a large one, was that he made at least one big mistake and possibly more. This is clear in the text. The diary requires very little explanation except the following two points.

Number one, his name was not Jack Faust. Another Slav scurrying westward dropped half the letters from the dozen of his name and in doing so earned a permanent place in English literature (would anyone seriously believe a man called Korzeniowski capable of writing a story called "Because of the Dollars"?). I have taken that hint and expunged his real name and, on the advice of my present editor, adopted this crisp two-syllable alias. It is intentionally symbolic: a *jack* is used to hoist a heavy object; he is *Jack*, the object a weighty truth he was too simple to grasp wholly. For consistency I will neither name the country nor the prison in which this diary was written. This will not confuse anyone. Western readers are not unfamiliar with this prison, despite its edited anonymity. Our dungeons are as familiar to students of Eastern European political fortunes as our boarded up synagogues are to anxiously vocal Western Jews who have never set foot in our country (name-calling is easy at that distance!). One has the impression that any regular reader of the current crop of frenzied memoirs by ex-Bolsheviks ("The man of steel took me on his lap and cooed, 'My little sparrowchik'") would have no difficulty at all finding his way about in a penal colony in Pskov, though he would probably become irretrievably lost in the rather grand Moscow metro or the modern Warsaw sink works. Even a dispirited and disaffected Party hack like myself is appalled by the general ignorance in the West of my country's achievements: sharp new flats have replaced cheesy peasant cottages, to name but one. Progress is progress; one should not hate the jackboot so much that one fails to notice whether it is down at the heel or making great strides. And simply because I was never given a chance to mention these things on television does not make them untrue.

Number two, what follows is a translation of the photographed manuscript I carried to America at great personal risk and sacrifice. I won't rub it in. No more explanation is in order. I can vouch for the truth of every word that "Jack Faust" wrote and for the gaumlessness with which he set each down. I can see him licking his pencil lead and scribbling, scribbling.

12 Nov.   I have committed no crime, but today I was arrested. My arm is still stiff from being twisted. I cannot write any more now except <u>I am innocent</u>. And this, though my hand pains me, I underline.

13 Nov.   My arm still hurts.

14 Nov.   Better. It happened in this way. Two burly secret policemen in shiny boots and well-cared-for truncheons beat at my door at five A.M. and told me to get dressed. I offered them buns. They refused saying, "This is not a social call, Comrade Faust. We are here on Party business." I asked one to pass me my new felt boots. "You won't be doing much walking where you're going," he said, and with that he kicked them out of my reach. As it turns out they would have come in quite handy. It is true I am in a small cell and do not walk much; but my feet are cold and I miss those boots. I hope Madam Zloty found them when she came to tidy up and had the good sense to pass them on to the chauffeur. The dopes will probably sell them, in which case I have the feeling the boots will eventually end up here: there seems to be quite a bit of black marketeering in this prison. Last night a voice whispered through the high window, "Cigarettes, chewing gum, razor blades." A small boy's voice, but I thought of Marushka with her little tray and her pathetic bunny costume and how she was so grateful when I befriended her. I mocked her crucifix and taught her to love the Party. If only she could see what the Party has done to me! And yet ... and yet I find it hard to believe that the committee knows of this. Surely this is a trick. They are testing me. I make no observation except the following: it is said that the Marquis de Sade wrote *Justine* in prison on a roll of toilet paper. This strikes me as incredible. Mine is already coming to bits under the flint of my stubby pencil, and I am hardly past square one.

15 Nov. The warder's name has a familiar ring. "Comrade Goldpork doesn't allow reading in this prison," the guard said when he saw me looking over some scraps of newspaper I found in the ticking of my mattress. "Goldpork, Goldpork," I murmured, shredding the newspaper, "I know that name." I believe we were in the Youth Wing together. He used to slouch horribly, a poor specimen of a Youth Winger. How I remember him being shouted at by the Platoon Commander! "Pig! Dog! Twist of dogshit!" the P. C. called at him. Goldpork stiffened under this abuse. Of course he could make no reply. A Youth Winger simply does not slouch. He stands straight as a ramrod; he snaps his salutes; he keeps his knickers in good order; he assiduously oils his truncheon. He coldly reports the activities of his grasping parents and notes how many pounds of lard have been hoarded by his mother. The Youth Wing is the backbone of the Party. Goldpork slouched and so was given the job of looking after this shabby penitentiary while I was composing rather hush-hush memoranda for B. And Goldpork doesn't allow reading! I wonder if he himself can read? The guard gave the order so stupidly (Can he know who I am?). I am not surprised Goldpork never got further than this prison. If I had my way he would be scrubbing the toilets—that is, all the toilets except the one in which I scribble this!

17 Nov. Just to while away the time I have spent the past day and a half itemizing a clean-up and renovation memorandum. I haven't lost my touch.

Memo to Goldpork

(a) As this is not a fish tank surely moss and fungus are not needed to keep the inmates well and happy. Scrape those tiles and make them shine.

(b) In my day, guards clicked their heels and polished their boots; the fact that guards are seen by no one but detainees should not excuse sloppy habits. Look smart.

(c) Note that chamberpots are designed for easy emptying. It is axiomatic that the full chamberpot overflows.

(d) There is an accumulation of rust on every iron bar in this prison. Prisoners should be made to feel that this is *their* prison as much as it is every citizen's. A sense of pride and purpose is wanted; a rust-scrubbing session with wire brushes would do wonders for morale. Let's buckle down.

(e) We have noted a preponderance of nightly comings and goings of small boys in frocks. This seems a questionable way of passing an evening. Must moral fiber necessarily break down because a man is behind bars? Work, cold showers, and honest fatigue: such things build the Party.

(f) We would like to see more prunes on the menu.

(g) If reading is not allowed, surely the ticking of all prison mattresses should be winnowed for bits of newspaper. This is a sensible measure: any of these newspapers may have reports of past events which have since proved to be malicious fabrications. We know many news items have been planted by foreign spies. Here, it is possible they will fall into the wrong hands. Sift, winnow, purge; get straw in those mattresses.

(h) Laughter. Why in the world are prisoners allowed to laugh and shriek? A more somber note could be struck if each laugh were awarded five of the best. Experience has shown a yard of bamboo to be most useful for this.

(i) The bindery is a shambles, a positive disgrace. We would like to see those glue pots kept in better order.

(j) The inspections are a joke.

The above are noted in a spirit of cooperation, with the following in mind: a good prison is a clean one; no one will accuse the warder of being soft because he wants to run "a tight ship." Skimping will not do. The habits of youth are carried into middle age; there is a definite slouch about this place.

(signed) *J. Faust*

23 Nov.   Have decided not to send the above to Goldpork as he may take it amiss and think I am trying to tell him how to do his job. I could send him memos until I was blue in the face and he would not pay any attention to me. When I am out of here he will have a lot of questions to answer. I shall keep my memo safe. I have submitted my request to see the minister of internal affairs when he makes his tour of this prison. I'll give him an earful!

24 Nov.   Why didn't I think of this before? The guard's words were, "No books, no papers, no pencils, no writing tablets." In my haste a few days ago I wrote something about Goldpork "not allowing reading"—probably for brevity's sake. I should have remembered the order. It was almost certainly Minute 345/67ZB in the Prisons Ordinance, Appendix D. I wrote that myself after we caught that Jew with his volume of reminiscences stuffed in his phylactery. And here I am giving Goldpork all the credit for it.

(later) The reason it all comes back to me is the typist. We worked late at the ministry that evening finishing up odds and ends of Party business. I was a stickler for detail, I wanted those minutes letter-perfect. I saw her slowing down, mumbling and erasing.

"Dinner?" I said, looking up from a foolscap file.

She turned away from her heavy black Yalor Office Console and flexed her fingers.

I snapped open my briefcase and handed her a sausage, a bit of bread, a cold potato. Gratefully she took them and, munching them, told me something about herself. I don't remember a word she said, but I recall thinking, "Yes, with a girl like that we have succeeded. Strong as a mule. Her tits are like turnips. She types a good rate and works like a dog. In the West she would be a frump at twenty."

Nor was typing her only talent.

I begin to understand these handsome little striplings mincing through the night corridors of this dungeon.

27 Nov. *Cement* did very well, ten editions in a year. And *Logs* was to do even better. Those two secret policemen interrupted me halfway through *Spindles.* I wonder if they destroyed the fragment of manuscript I kept on my writing table? No, I don't wonder at all. They did, of course they did. To do otherwise would have been a flagrant disregard of their orders. They had a duty to perform. Is it bourgeois of me to hope that before those pages were incinerated some soul read them and had doubts about my guilt?

30 Nov. Find this notebook, Goldpork! Here is one manuscript you won't unearth. I write nearly every day, squatting on this bucket in your unclean stall. You would never think to look here! You have not discovered me, and until you reform this prison you never shall! I am noting this under your very nose! Pig! Dog!

2 Dec. The minister's visit was brusquely announced for the first of December. I handed in my chit and said that I would like a word with him in private. "I know my rights," I said. I walked on eggshells all day, with the crumpled squares of the Memo to Goldpork tucked into the elastic of my underpants. No minister. I waited all day today. No minister.

3 Dec. No minister.

4 Dec. No minister.

5 Dec. No minister.

6 Dec. What this country needs is a good solid overhaul by some merciless but farsighted Party man. When a minister announces a visit he has made a promise; this promise must be kept. The Memo to Goldpork of 17 Nov. is all but deteriorated in my underpants. I shall recopy it while waiting for the minister. I am not surprised Goldpork kept his job for so long. He would not last a minute in my charge.

7 Dec. No minister. I shall put the memo squares with the rest of this little diary. That minister is asking for a sacking.

8 Dec. "It was like battling with a pillow. Squeezed at one end it bulged at the other..." (*Cement*, Ch. 10). I was writing of the landlords and moneylenders and the bullies in the ballroom. I could have been writing of my present difficulties.

Item: Enemies

(1) Goldpork
(2) The minister of internal affairs
(3) Fatso, G's toad
(4) The little chap who visited me several nights ago and played hard to get

9 Dec. The film version of *Logs* was praised and won a coveted medal. It opened with a panorama of a great banqueting hall. Fat men slobbering over pigs' trotters, ladies yelling, young men reaching into the bosoms of dowagers, dogs lapping up scraps. The camera moved to the cellar of the house: bearded old men reclining in coal piles, little boys whimpering. Back to the banqueting hall: fat men begin to dance with one another. Jigs and reels. "Spin the floor!" cries one man (close shot of hairy face, hog jowls, foodflecked fangs). He stamps on the floor with his big boots. Cut below to cellar: old men and young boys putting on harnesses; they begin to tug and yank, like cattle on a threshing floor. Above, the people dance, the floor revolves gently; music plays. Fat men clutch their partners' bums. "Faster! Faster!" they call; they stamp. Below, the proletariat get the message. They summon all their strength; they run in their harnesses: they are literally dancing. The old men become young, the young men strong. Above, the floor is spinning, revolving crazily, much too fast. The first fat man falls, then another. A dowager sprawls and spills her pearls. Skirts fly. The dancers are spun from the revolving floor by centrifugal force; some are knocked cold. Below, the workers strip off their harnesses and sing. A small boy makes a fist and raises his arm. Last shot: this dirty little fist.

I used to know what all this represented. I am not so sure now.

10 Dec. Clearly, the inner Party has gone soft. My analogy is the potato raked out of the coals too soon. Break open that crusty jacket, dig your fork into the soft mealy white . . . but *wait*! Grasp the potato with two hands and pinch it open: a cold hard center will be revealed. Burned on the outside, but cold and uncooked at the center . . . and that indigestible lump is enough to ruin the whole meal.

In our discussions, particularly at the Twentieth Plenum, we decided on and minuted the reverse of this. It was, so to say, the center of the potato we were certain was nourishing; we were not so sure of the rest.

Problem: Identify the potato's components, the fire, the tongs.

Who eats this potato?

There are rumors flying about. They say the minister has come and gone. But how could he? He hasn't seen me. He is fiddling his mileage claim, there is no doubt of that.

Ask yourself, Comrade Minister, which Party member penned the second Five-Year Plan? Yes, I wear manacles, but none of my chains weighs as heavily as this ingratitude.

11 Dec. Are there compensations here? Yes, I confess there are. Today, during our ten-minute fresh-air stroll we clanked as usual in a circle, reminding me of the painting by that insane Dutchman of a prison scene—blue convicts in a blue exercise yard—a painting, let me record, hanging in the Pushkin Museum in Moscow (who said the Russians are an insensitive people?). And one, then another and another of my fellow prisoners whispered hoarsely, "That's him! There he is!" This continued ("That's *him*!") until the guard knocked one of the whispers to the ground and told him to pipe down. But they continued to look at me with their gray faces. Several lifted their chains at me and shook them. It's nice to be recognized in a crowd.

14 Dec.   At night now they scream my name.

15 Dec.   They're still doing it. It gives me quite a lift.

16 Dec.   Today I was set upon by six inmates and beaten. It was just after breakfast while we were emptying our chamberpots into the swill vat. The guards stand as far away as possible (the stink is overpowering) and these six, seeing their chance, gagged me with a mitten and knocked me insensible. I was not found until half-past ten. I was given broth and told to report to Goldpork. He recognized me immediately.

"Comrade Faust, we meet again."

"Under less happy circumstances than before, Goldpork, I don't have to remind you."

"Sit down, I want to have a word with you. What's this I hear about the stir you're causing in your cellblock?"

"They scream my name. I liked it at first, but today they beat me. They dug their fingers into my eyes and plucked at my neck and cheeks. I hated it."

"And what do you conclude from this little affair?"

"Simple. They belong here. I don't. You know, Goldpork, we built this prison for them, not for ourselves. It is they who should be munching on scraps and wiping the rims of their soiled chamberpots . . . not me. If only I had known!"

"You didn't deserve to be beaten, then? Don't you see that these men are relatives of all the people you liquidated?"

"I have one regret. I should have searched the houses more carefully. I might have turned up one or two of these oafs in cupboards and liquidated them as well."

"And so you're trying to tell me you are a faithful Party member still?"

"I have committed no crime. I am not one of these comrades who runs shrieking into the arms of a Western publisher as soon as I am wronged, though I know I could live quite a nice little life if I did that. But I am not one of your backsliders. I was put in here, and here I will stay until the Party feels I have been punished enough. When I am set free I will work as always, with fervor."

"It's pleasant to hear that, Comrade Faust. You bear us no ill will?"

"None at all."

But I had. Though I only realized it after I went back to my cell and reread all the entries in this diary. I was dreadfully afraid. I held these scraps of paper up to the light and, as my name boomed through the corridors, I read with a sinking heart. I begin by saying I am innocent. I go on to complain about Goldpork and itemize ten objections to this prison. I slander the minister and the guard. I indulge in bourgeois nostalgia about my tenth-rate film. And as if this is not enough six days ago I describe the Inner Party as a lump of underdone potato.

Furthermore, and much worse, I withheld all of this from Goldpork. I tried to pass myself off as a good Party member. But what is a good Party member doing in prison? I had said when I pocketed my Party card that I would serve. I am doing nothing of the sort. I am a complainer, like the chap on the commune who won't dig sugar beets because his mattock is bent. I should have told Goldpork exactly where I stood. If I were honest I would hand over this diary. What earthly good is it? It represents nothing. Who would bother to read it except one of our magistrates or those Western publishers? It is an indulgence. I will write no more today.

17 Dec.   Spent the whole day poking through my mattress looking for reactionary newspaper clippings to read. Found nothing. Knock on door. Fatso. Asked what pile of straw and oakum on floor might be. Told him to his face.

Note: Delete (g), (h) and (j) from Memo to Goldpork. These have apparently been remedied while I was busy

with this diary. They know what they are doing. This is
further evidence that I am a scab. It was no trick. My
guilt shows in every square I fill. After this knowledge,
what forgiveness?

24 Dec. There is some satisfaction, when in prison, in
knowing that one is guilty. The time passes quickly, one
stops talking to oneself, one bears no grudges. I look
forward to seeing Goldpork again and telling him everything, perhaps producing this diary from my shirt front
and letting it spill over his desk. They were right all along.
My imagined innocence weighed on me and made me lax;
but, guilty, I have a place—I belong. I see the logic of
their decision to thump on my door with truncheons and
drag me bootless from my flat. Today I sat and mused,
humming a tune I once heard with Marushka when we
secretly listened—as we did countless times!—to the
broadcast of a foreign power. I am not Party material,
and it is clear that Goldpork is. I shall see him tomorrow
and cheerfully convey my guilt by wishing him a Merry
Christmas.

Those were the last words Jack Faust was to write. He
handed over his diary and freely confessed to all his
crimes. They were mostly imaginary ones, but they con-
tained such a wild note of threat that he was hanged before
the new year. He was not mourned. I know this is true.
My reward for extracting his confession from him—I did
little more than listen to him and nod to the steno—was
a very agreeable posting in Rome, attached to our embassy; my job was to round up people who had fled the
country and were seeking asylum in Italy. I got to know
the ins and outs of fleeing, and I was helped in my searches
by Marushka, whose full name and address I had found
scratched on the wall of Jack's cell. In our six months in
Rome we drugged many an escapee and posted each back
to the capital in a mailbag. Only Marushka could have
been expected to mourn Jack Faust, yet when I asked
her she denied all knowledge of him. I could only smile.
    And smiling one night I said I was stepping out for a
breath of fresh air. I did so and never returned. The morning I left Italy (this was in Milan) I thought I saw Marushka

whiz past me, straddling the back of a Vespa and clutching the Italian driver with one hand and what I believe was the manuscript of Jack's unfinished novel (*Spindles*) with the other. But I may be wrong; many Italian girls had Marushka's knees, and all girls jounce the same on a scooter: I love to see their rolling bottoms and hear the seat springs oink! In any case, Marushka is doing all right for herself. I am pretty sure she pinched *Spindles* from Jack's flat; I know I never discovered what happened to it. The police were no help. I have a feeling that one of these days I'm going to see it in translation on the revolving paperback bookstand at my corner drugstore.

During our last conversation Jack had a moment of panic. He saw the toilet roll of his whole incriminating diary spread out on my desk and said, "Wait, Goldpork, I'll make a deal with you!" I flapped my hand and brushed aside the terms he was stammering at me. I said, "But don't you see you've already made one?" Then the guards appeared and led him away. I had not finished speaking. I wanted to say that we all make deals. It is a pity he did not live long enough to see that mine at least had a reasonably happy ending.

A REAL RUSSIAN IKON

▲▲▲▲▲▲▲▲▲▲▲▲▲▲▲▲▲▲▲▲▲▲▲▲▲▲▲▲▲

FRED HAGBERG, FOREWARNED BY HIS TRAVEL AGENT IN Cleveland of the Russian hunger for hard cash, had been in Moscow for two days and there had not been even a glimmer of interest in his dollars. The plastic cover of his American Express wallet stayed buttoned; Intourist paid all the bills. He expected to be guided to seedy black-market shops off the beaten track or, at the very least, pestered for cigarettes and Chiclets. There wasn't a peep from the Muscovites, and Fred thought maybe his travel agent meant somewhere else.

On the evening of the third day he was ambling along Karl Marx Prospekt, where it runs into Manège Square, returning from the Palace of Congresses where he had seen Verdi hysterically acted and shrieked to an audience of cows. The Mob of Shuffling Humanity, he called them, as they slushed along the sidewalk in felt boots, oblivious of everything, ignoring everything, tramping nowhere into the night. Fred hated their guts. He had just turned away from the revolting sight of two Russians eating (eating! on the sidewalk! at night!) when it happened.

There was a voice, the thickened tongue lap of the impossible language, audible but disembodied. Fred

17

looked down. A small boy in a blue Bolshevik beanie, hands crammed into the pockets of a capelike coat, lurched alongside him. The boy was looking away, looking around in the direction of a slapping banner which, secured by cables, was being driven against the trolley wires by the wind and making sparks.

"Cherman?"

The boy turned from the slapping banner to the Obelisk to Revolutionary Thinkers, peered at the spikes and spoke again.

"Enklis?"

"American," said Fred.

"Unidestates?"

Fred nodded and blew on his hands. He saw that the boy was still avoiding his gaze, looking distractedly elsewhere, slouching along the salt-gritty sidewalk, the perfection of KGB aplomb, furtive but at the same time very cool.

The next exchange took Fred a while to understand, for each time the boy spoke he looked away. The boy apparently wanted chewing gum: Fred had none. The boy wanted a ball-point pen (he called it a "pall-boint"): Fred said yes. He fingered his Parker Jotter. The boy turned sharply right and headed toward a newspaper kiosk, closed up for the night. Fred followed.

In the glare of the sputtering arc lamp high above, Fred saw in the boy's palm a small enamel pin stamped with the gold head of Lenin and the dates *1917–1967*. "Nice medal, good, best," said the little boy. "For the pen."

"Deal," said Fred, offering it.

The boy took a deep breath, rolled his eyes up, prodded the Parker up his sleeve and, turning away, deftly passed the little pin to Fred. The blue beanie disappeared into the darkness at the steps that led to 25th October Street, behind the Ploshchad Revolutsii Metro entrance.

Back at the Metropole Hotel, in a room heated to a skin-crinkling eighty, Fred flicked on the fake chandelier and examined the pin. He knew, with that certainty that comes quickly to travelers, that he had been swindled. He ground it into the squares of shrunken parquet with his heel, and then spat.

* * *

Over a breakfast of syrupy coffee and flaking pastry Fred collected his thoughts. He had not, he decided, lost completely: a deal had been made. Only shrewdness had been missing, and that on his part. He had been too eager. Furthermore he had been dealing with a kid. But several things stood out in the incident, and these were important: the Russians made deals, they talked to foreigners, and they were cagey. Pondering these Russian qualities Fred missed the English Speakers' tour of the city. There was only one thing left, something Fred had counted on seeing: the graveyard of the Novodevichy Convent, where Svetlana's mother was buried. She was the lady, mentioned in the *Twenty Letters*, to whom Stalin had called, "Hey you!" and who, miffed, had gone upstairs and shot herself.

The taxi stand was at Sverdlovsky Square, near the Bolshoi Theater. A long line of people, laden with fishnet shopping bags (some showing withered fruit), stood morosely in mangy fur hats and ankle-length overcoats. Their noses glowed red, redder than the flags on the light poles or the banners on the Bolshoi which praised the Komsomol for fifty years of tireless devotion.

Fred fumbled for a cigarette with cold hands. He picked open the crushed pack of Luckies and withdrew a bent one. Smoothing it slowly, he felt subtle pressure on his sides, two warm bears, then a voice, a steamy word.

"Enklis?"

"United States," said Fred, squirming, feeling for his wallet of traveler's checks. He smelled pickpockets.

"Amerikansk?"

"Yeah," said Fred, looking up into a raw knobby face.

"Toureest?"

"Mm."

Without moving a muscle Fred felt himself turning in the taxi line, revolving on an axis like a slow-motion soldier. Again, without any effort on his part, he was borne by the pressure of the two bears to the near sidewalk where the giant seated figure of Ostrovsky in bronze brooded over a bird-limed manuscript.

Shortly, they were in a tearoom, the Uyut (Cozy) on Leninsky Prospekt, exchanging names. The bears were Igor and Nikolai and, by way of introduction, said they liked Willis Conover, someone Fred had never heard of, though Igor insisted he was a great American. Other names were dropped—Jim Reeves, the Beatles, Dave Brubeck, Jack London, President Kennedy—and then they got down to business.

"Dollars?"

"You mean, do I have dollars?"

"To have dollars," said Nikolai.

"Sure, I've got everything. I'm going around the world on the Pan Am flight. Pan American. You know what I mean?"

"American dollars. Very nice," said Igor. "You want rubles?"

"I want an ikon," said Fred. And added, "For my mother."

Neither Russian understood.

"Ikon, ikon, ikon."

Nikolai mumbled to Igor, whose face brightened. "You want *eekone?*"

Fred nodded. It seemed useless to speak.

"Eekone," said Nikolai. He giggled.

"We find eekone, you pay dollars us," said Igor. "To want rubles."

"It's got to be a good one. A *good one.*"

"Don't whorry."

They were in a battered taxi, Fred in the back seat with Nikolai, the silent one. Igor, taller, more garrulous, sat in front with the driver, giving instructions. Down the wide avenues they sped, jockeying through the traffic, the little taxi slipping between a Zyl and a Zym, two tanklike cars resembling old Packards, complete with chrome jaws. They drew up to a shop that looked like a pawn-broker's, where Igor fought to the front of a mob of people around a counter and shouted the familiar word. A shop-girl folded her arms across her smock and shook her head.

At another similar place a shopgirl pointed to an inferior painting on the wall depicting a muscular bleeding Christ. Igor looked questioningly at Fred. Fred said, "*Nyet.*"

The taxi driver seemed to take an interest in the search. He muttered to Igor; Igor muttered back; Nikolai emitted a cluck, sucking at his front teeth, the sound that in most of Europe means yes. They were off again, and from the way the Russians settled back in their seats it looked as if it was going to be a long ride. They passed under the red banners which Fred drew their attention to. When they saw that Fred was interested they read each one—quite a feat, since there were three to a block and the taxi was going fast.

"Great Russian People," said Igor, pointing. "Good Komsomol Fifty Year . . . Hail Russian Worker." He interspersed the banners with sales talk as well: "Work Hard . . . Dollars very nice . . . Build State . . . Cash or check? . . . Remember Comrade Lenin . . . We find real Russian eekone . . . Crush Imperialism . . ."

They rode for several miles more, into a dingy suburb squeezed with old one-story houses. The eaves of these houses were carved, but all were in disrepair. The taxi parked on the sidewalk. The driver got out, shouted something to Igor, and then disappeared through a gray wooden door. Fred made a move to get up, but Igor waved him back.

"Nice scarf," Igor finally said.

"This one?" Fred fingered his scarf.

"Sell?"

"I need it. It's cold here."

"Ten rubles, fifty kopeks."

"I want an ikon, an ikon! I *need* this scarf. It's cold—"

Igor stirred. The driver was giving a signal from the doorway of the ramshackle house. "We go," said Igor.

Fred was allowed to go in first. On entering, he did not notice the old lady, but when his eyes grew accustomed to the darkness he saw her—small, pale, standing fretfully among draped furniture, her white hair appearing in several tendrils from under her shawl. Her facial skin was loose and wrinkled, as if she had once been fat, the skin stretched and retaining its former size. Her eyebrows were heavy, her hands were large, she wore three sweaters and appeared much afraid.

Igor addressed the old lady. In the conversation that went on Fred heard the word *Amerikansk* again. The second time he heard it he smiled at the old lady, who looked incredulous for a moment, then stepped closer to Fred and smiled. It was an open, trusting smile which revealed her small fine teeth and creased her whole face like an old apple. She spoke to Fred in Russian.

"She asking you to want tea. She have her brother in America."

"Look, I didn't come here for tea," said Fred. The old lady implored him with an odd grace. "Okay, I'll have a cup of tea."

A smoking, steaming samovar was brought. It was brass and, even in that dingy room stuffed with junk, gleamed like a church fixture. A small valve at the top popped open, shooting jets of steam into the chill air. The old lady placed a teapot under the spigot and twisted the key: hot water bubbled out. There were no wires anywhere.

Fred smacked his lips. "That's some contraption!"

"You like?" It was Igor, smiling like a cat and rubbing his hands.

"How much?"

The smile left Igor's face. He turned to the old lady who, when Igor spoke, shut the hot water off and looked quickly at Fred. She showed her large gnarled hands, shrugged and said several words.

"No sell, she say."

"I'll give her fifty dollars." Fred began flashing fingers at the old lady, two hands at a time, ten, twenty, thirty . . .

"*Karasho*," said Igor impatiently, "Okay, okay." He spoke again, his voice rising, his eyeballs rolling. The old lady muttered another reply and drew her shawl tighter.

"She want. For tea. No sell."

"Oh, for God's sake," said Fred. "Listen, for fifty bucks she can buy *two* of them, electric ones, any kind she wants. Doesn't she want a nice electric one?"

Nikolai said nothing. He simply snatched up a candle and wagged it in Fred's face, giving Fred a crazy grin that said, "No electricity—isn't it awful?"

"Okay, forget it."

But he wanted his trophy. The faint stamp in his passport CCCP, MOCKBA and a date was not enough. Something substantial was needed, like the *bierstein*, the rosary, the blue Wedgwood pot. And even if he could not be the traveler who brought home a demure full-breasted peasant girl, he would have his modest souvenir. If not, what was the sense in coming so far? And to Russia, no less.

In silence, the tea was drunk. Fred finished his first. He placed his chipped cup on the floor and said, "What about the ikon? I haven't got all day."

"Eekone, yes."

The three Russian men gathered around the old lady. Igor did all the talking, pointing to Fred and, once, asking the taxi driver's opinion. While he spoke Fred saw a vivid moment in his mind, a very familiar one: he was back in Cleveland with his pals and they were making a deal. The faces were eager, joshing American ones, reddish, large nosed, rough. The Russians even had crew cuts, the same thick ears and deep wrinkles. They were grinning and pushy-looking in a Midwestern way. They even seemed to be yakking in English!

The sight of the worn carpet, the sheets over the furniture, the coldness of the room, brought Fred back to reality. He was halfway around the world from Cleveland, in enemy territory. He reminded himself to be careful.

The discussion was still going on, the old lady appearing not to understand. She asked many questions and got many shrugs, many gestures, many little sharp cries of admonishment as replies. Then the old lady rose very reluctantly, with sighs, and beckoned Fred into a little room at the side. The room was damp and even darker than the outer parlor. It was hung with heavy tapestries which, when the old lady lit a candle, appeared to be delicately embroidered. The room had the eerie glow of a chapel; in fact, the candle was in a red glass chimney on a gold-wrought stand. It was a vigil light and could have come from a very large church.

Warming the wax, the candle flared up. Above it gleamed the ikon, a painting the size of an airline calendar, Mary and child with tiny carefully made faces and thin hands. Each head wore a coronet of little sparkling gems; in places there were pocks where gems had been. And Fred noticed that the paint had cracked, the boards had warped, the cloth around the frame had frayed. Still, it was beautiful. The candle flame grew higher, picking out tiny cherubs with trumpets, lilies, roses and fishes, scrolls and, at the top of the ikon, a wordy motto in elongated characters like gold washing hung on a line.

"Boy," said Fred.

"You like?" asked Igor. To Nikolai he said, "He like." Nikolai grunted.

"Is good," said Igor, turning to Fred. "Is nice Russian eekone."

"How much?" asked Fred.

"Is good eekone," Igor replied. "Not much. Three hundred."

"Rubles?"

"Dollars."

"Two fifty," said Fred.

"Okay. Two fifty."

Fred cursed himself for not saying two hundred. "Traveler's checks?"

"Is better dollars cash."

"I don't carry that kind of money around in cash," said Fred obstinately. "So it's traveler's checks or nothing. You understand? *Traveler's checks!*"

Igor winced. Fred realized he had shouted in the little chapel; he apologized. The apology seemed to bewilder them more than the offense.

"Ask her if it's okay."

Igor sidled up to the old lady and spoke, flicking his finger at the ikon. At Igor's words the old lady drew away, her back to the little altar, as if protecting it. She clapped her hands to her mouth, stifling a shriek; then, petrified, she wagged her head rigidly from side to side.

"No sell," said Igor, inexplicably grinning.

"No sell," mumbled Fred. "Did you tell her the price?"

"Now I tell." Igor shot fingers into the old lady's face and, at the same time, brayed numbers.

The old lady lowered her eyes and shook her head in a gentle negative.

Fred understood. "Not enough, eh? Fine, how much does she want for it?"

The old lady glanced up at Fred and spoke quickly. Her head dropped once more.

Grinning in the manner of Igor, Nikolai blessed himself

with the sign of the cross, finishing by kissing his bitten finger tips.

"She wants. For pray," said Igor.

"What?"

Igor blessed himself as Nikolai had done, but Igor did it with his left hand and cast his eyes up to the ikon. Fred looked at the taxi driver. He smiled sheepishly and did the same.

"What! Are you *kidding* me? Listen, you people don't pray—it's against the law, for God's sake. Listen..." Fred knew he was talking too fast for the Russians. He tried in broken English: "Communist no like church. Huh? Church very bad. Praying bad. Priests bad. No pray in Soviet Union. Huh?" His patience was exhausted. He went on angrily, "So what the hell is this old lady talking about, will you just tell me that?"

Igor got the point. He leered. "Komsomol no like this." He clapped his hands prayerfully under his chin and attempted an appearance of devotion.

"Right. Tell *her* that," Fred said coldly.

Igor began to speak, but was interrupted by Fred again. "And tell her," Fred went on, "that she'll get into trouble if she keeps on praying, because it's against the law. And you know what *that* means! Siberia, right? Right. Go ahead, tell her."

"Is good idea," said Igor. He tapped the side of his head and puckered his mouth appreciatively, as if to say, "Good thinking." And then he spoke to the old lady. He had not said ten words when the old lady looked fearfully at Fred and sucked in her breath. She seemed trapped, as if the floor of the fragile chapel was about to give way and drop her onto a rock pile. She started to protest, but broke off in the middle of a word and wept. She averted her eyes from the four men in the room; she stared at the frayed carpet and, taking the knotted end of her shawl into her mouth, bit it, the way a person being tortured tries to endure pain. She moaned.

"Tell her to cut that out!" said Fred. She seemed to be doing it on account of him, pretending it was all his fault. He began to hate the old lady for making him feel that way. "All right," Fred finally said, "no deal. The deal's off. I don't want it! Will you tell her to cut it out!"

Fred was now shouting louder than the old lady was crying. It had a chastening effect on her; her sobbing died to a sniffle.

Igor spoke and, as he did, the old lady continued to sniff. "She wants sell eekone very much." He winked. "Two hundred fifty dollars, American."

"But I thought you said—"

"Wants sell to you," Igor said. He stood near Nikolai and the taxi driver. Their faces were triumphantly rosy.

"Doesn't she want it for praying?"

Igor translated with evident malice.

The old lady looked at Fred with red eyes full of pleading fear, more fear than she had shown toward the three Russians. Her voice was small, her face puffy with grief, her unusually large arthritic-knuckled hands clenched tightly over her knees.

"She no pray. She say to me, *No pray, comrade!*"

In the men's toilet of the Uyut tearoom Fred coated his hands with slimy Soviet soap and scalded them in the sink while a customer kecked into the commode. At last the customer left. Fred and Igor made the final transaction. Fred passed the traveler's checks wadded in brutally heavy toilet paper to Igor who reached under the gap in the wall of an adjoining water closet.

Outside, at their table, the deal complete, they touched teacups.

"Chin-chin," said Igor.

"Wait a minute, wait a minute, wait a minute," said Fred, feeling oddly abandoned and fearful. "What am I going to tell them at the customs desk at the airport? They're going to ask me where I got this thing." The bundle lay beside Fred's chair, innocuous-looking in *Pravda* and old twine. Fred pointed cautiously, then cupped his hands to his mouth and whispered, "I'll get into trouble. They'll know I changed my money illegally." Fred looked to Igor for reassurance. "I don't want any trouble."

"No trouble," said Igor.

"What do you mean—"

Igor hushed him; people at other tables had turned to watch the man shouting in English.

"What," said Fred with pained hoarseness, "do you mean, no trouble? They're looking for people who've changed their money on the black market. I'm an American, for God's sake, *an American!* They'll lock me up. I know they will." Fred was inconsolable. He sighed. "I *knew* this whole thing was a mistake."

Igor chuckled. "No trouble. Tell police this eekone present."

"Sure, a present. You're a great help."

"Present, yes," Igor said calmly. "Find young policeman. Young man. Tell him, heh, you fack Russian gorl. She say, heh, yes, very good, thank you. Gorl give you eekone as present for fack. Easy."

"Oh, my God."

"Don't whorry." Igor winked. "We go." He took Nikolai by the arm and departed, leaving Fred to pay the bill.

Fred was upset. Walking back to the Metropole he decided to throw the ikon away and forget the whole business. The decision calmed him, but he grew tense when he realized there was nowhere to throw the ikon. The alleys were bare; there was not a scrap of rubbish or even a trash can on any of the streets. The gutters were being scrubbed by old women in shawls with big brushes. The bundle would be noticed as a novelty (no one threw anything away in Moscow) and would attract attention.

It was all the more worrying for Fred when the elevator operator, a sullen, wet-lipped man in a faded braided uniform, gave the bundle cradled in Fred's arm a very queer look. Fred shoved it under his bed, downed three neat vodkas and went to the Bolshoi to see *The Tsar's Bride*. He had been cheated on the tickets: he sat behind a post in the sixty-kopek heights, in the darkness, shredding his program with anxious hands.

That night he could not sleep. The haggard face of the old lady appeared in his room. She accused him of stealing her valuable ikon. A Russian policeman with a face like raw mutton tore Fred's passport in half and twisted his arm. Igor, in a chair under a bright light, confessed everything. Nikolai wept piteously and pointed an accusing finger at Fred. Toward dawn Fred lapsed into feverish sleep. He awoke with a vow on his lips.

It was not easy for him to find the old lady's house. The banners were some help in figuring the general direction, but it was not until a day and a half after the visit with Igor and Nikolai—one day before he was due to leave for Tokyo—that he found the right street.

He rapped hard at the gray door, so hard he skinned some leather from his glove knuckles. He soon saw why there was no answer: a heavy padlock clinked in a hasp at the bottom of the door. Turning, Fred was brought up short by a figure on the sidewalk, standing with his hands in his pockets, eyeing him closely.

"Do you speak English?"

"If you zpeak zlowly."

"Where is the old lady?"

"Not here," said the man. At that moment a chauffered Zyl drew up to the curb. "You are friend?"

"In a way. See, a couple of days ago—"

"Come," said the man darkly.

They drove through narrow streets, then out to the wide Sadovaya that rings Moscow, and across the canal to more narrow gray streets, in the bare district of black stumps and boarded-up houses near the Church of the Assumption in Gonchary. They passed the church and continued for about half a mile over frost heaves in the empty street.

"Where are we?"

"Gvozdev," said the man, and he gave the driver a direction.

The car pulled in through a low gate cut in a thick stone wall. At the far end of a scrubby courtyard was a sooty brick building, the shape of Monticello on the back of the nickel, a domed roof but with one difference: this one had a chimney at the rear belching greasy smoke. It was too squat, too plain, too gloomy for a church. Fred pulled the ikon out of the car and followed the man into the building.

The front entrance—there were no doors—opened onto a vast, high-ceilinged room, empty of furniture. The walls were covered with small brown photographs of men and women, framed in silver and set into the cement, not

hung. The cold wind whistling through the front entrance
blew soot and grit into the faces of people milling about
in the center of the room. It was a silent group, apparently
workers; Fred saw that their eyes were fixed on three
men who sat on a raised platform at the far end.

The three men were dressed in long coats and boots.
They all wore gloves. This would not have seemed so
strange except that two of the men were holding violins;
the third was seated at an organ. They began to play, still
gloved, a mournful and aching song.

From a side door two men entered, carrying a coffin
which they set in front of the musicians' platform. One
of the pallbearers placed a small sprig of flowers on the
coffin and touched the wood with his fingers.

"Old lady," said the man next to Fred. "She die I am
not zurprised. It is formidable how she live zo long in this
cold."

The scraping of the violins and the heavy breathing of
the organ continued as the coffin descended into the floor,
accompanied by the steely clanking of a hidden chain.
The coffin bumped down and out of sight. Two trap doors
shot up, met and shut with a bang which echoed in the
stone room. When the echo died out the musicians
stopped playing and at once began tuning their instru-
ments.

"Say." Fred turned to the man. He cleared his throat.
"Can you direct me to the Novodevichy Convent?" He
said nothing about Svetlana. There might have been trouble. On the other hand he felt sure he would get the ikon
past customs now.

A POLITICAL ROMANCE

▲▲▲▲▲▲▲▲▲▲▲▲▲▲▲▲▲▲▲▲▲▲▲▲▲▲

To CALM HIS WIFE AFTER A QUARREL, MORRIS ROSETREE always recalled to her how they had met in the National Library in Prague, how he had said, "Excuse me, miss, could you tell me where the reading room is?" and how she had replied, "You are excused. It is in this vichinity."

He had been doing research for his doctoral dissertation on the history of the Czechoslovak Communist Party. But he had lost interest in it. He asked about the reading room because he heard it was well heated: he wanted to sit comfortably and write a letter to his folks. Several days after asking the dark-eyed girl the question he saw her on the library steps and he offered her a lift home. She refused at first, but Morris was insistent and finally he persuaded her. She remained silent, seemed to hold her breath throughout the journey. Morris invited her for coffee the next day, and later to have lunch. He told her he was an American. On Valentine's Day he bought her some fur-lined gloves. She was glad to get them, she said. She was an orphan. When they were married it was noticed by several American newspapers; one paper printed a picture of the bride and groom and titled it *A Political Romance*, explaining in the text that love was bigger than

politics. At that time very little was happening in Czechoslovakia: Morris Rosetree's marriage there to Lepska
Kanek was news.

With the help of Lepska, Morris finished his research.
A year later, in the States, Morris got his Ph.D., and he
told Lepska that if it hadn't been for her he would never
have managed it. Some chapters of the dissertation were
published in political journals, but no publisher seemed
interested in the whole book. What depressed Morris
some time after his book had been turned down was a
review he saw of a similar book. The review was enthu-
siastic ("... valuable, timely ..."), but judging from quo-
tations used in the review the book was no better than
his own. He knew his own was dull, so he was irritated
reading praise of a book equally dull on the same subject.
He became so discouraged that he moved away from Eastern European affairs and began a fitful study of the ruling
parties of certain African countries.

It was at about this time that his quarrels started with
Lepska who, once she had arrived at the Massachusetts
college, nicknamed herself Lil. Morris had found her accent attractive in the early years of their marriage: "You
could cut that accent with a knife." She had learned Morris' swearwords ("Kleist!" "Sanvabeach!"). Morris had
been charmed by her way of asking dinner guests innocently, "There was big—how do you say *rayseestonce*
in English?" (this provoked "Resistance!" from the
guests). But now the accent annoyed Morris. When she
said, "You Americans hev zoch dirty manners," he cor-
rected her English. If there were friends present he said,
"Sure, Americans have bad manners. Look at this. This
is the way your Czechs eat their grub." He reached across
the table, speared a potato on his fork and made noises
of chewing and growling as he cut the potato savagely on
his plate. The friends laughed. Lil went silent; her face
shut. Afterward she cried and said she was going back to
Prague with the children. They had two girls: one had
been born while Morris was finishing his dissertation; one
a year later. Both had Czech names. Lil cried in their
room.

"Remember the library?" Morris would say whenever
Lil cried. He could do both voices well, his bewildered

American question, her stiff mispronounced reply.

One night she rejected the memory and said bitterly, "I vish I had not met you."

"Aw, Lil."

"You make me zo unhappy," she sniffed. Then she shrieked, "I do not vant to leave!"

"Christ, I don't want you to either."

"No, not *leave* . . . leave!" she insisted, and burst into tears again.

She was, Morris guessed, talking of suicide.

He went easy on her for a while and was careful not to criticize her accent. But something had happened to the marriage: it had become impersonal; he felt they did not know each other very well, and he didn't care to know her any better. Her accent made him impatient and set his teeth on edge: he interrupted her as you do a stutterer. She moped like a hostage. Her hips were huge, her face and hands went florid in the January cold, though her face was still pretty. But she was like so many Czech women he had seen in Prague, like his landlady, like the librarians and the shrews in the ministries who would not allow him to interview officials. Those women who tried to kill his research: they wore brown, belted dresses and heavy shoes; not old in years, they were made elderly by work. Somehow, they were fat.

His daughters were fat, too, and once Morris had said to his office mate O'Hara (the Middle East), "I think if we gave them American names they'd get skinny again." O'Hara laughed. Morris was, afterward, ashamed of having revealed his exasperation. Exasperation was the name he gave it, despair was what he felt: because nothing would change for him. He would have no more kids; he would not marry again. He had tenure: this was his job for life. He could hope for promotion, but in thirty years he would be—this hurt him—the same man, if not a paler version. The manuscript of his book, the letters from publishers containing phrases of terse praise and regret and solemn rejection clipped to the flyleaf, would stay in the bottom drawer of his desk. Once he had had momentum and had breathed an atmosphere of expectancy; he had flown across Europe and been afraid. But he had been younger then, and a student, and he had been in love.

The study he planned of ruling parties was getting no-where. He could not keep up with the revolutions or the new names (the presidents and generals in these countries were so young!). He taught Political Theory and used a textbook that a colleague had written. Morris knew it was not a good one.

Then the Russians invaded Czechoslovakia. Morris looked at his newspaper and saw photographs of chaos. He was tempted to throw the paper away and pay no further attention, for he could not separate in his mind the country from that woman in his house (Lil!) urging food into the two fat little girls whose Slavic names, in-stead of being dimmed by three and four years of utter-ance, had acquired queer, unfamiliar highlights and were the roots of even sillier diminutives, encouraging ridicule.

Morris fought that impulse, and he did not want the oblique revenge which his indifference to the invasion would have been. So he read the story and looked at the pictures, and he felt exhilaration, anger stoked by a con-tinuous flow of indignant shame, as if he had returned to a deserted neighborhood and realized, standing amid abandoned buildings, that he too had been a deserter. The pictures were of Prague: tanks in formation on a thoroughfare's cobbles, their slender cannon snouts sniff-ing at rumpled citizens; some boys near the tanks with their hands cupped at their mouths, obviously shouting; others, reaching, in the act of pitching stones; people being chased into doorways by soldiers wearing compli-cated boots and carrying rifles; people laying wreaths; pathetically small crowds wagging signs; two old ladies, with white flowers, weeping. Morris read the news report and the editorial, and he fumbled with a cigarette, dis-covering as he puffed that he had put the wrong end in his mouth and lighted the filter tip.

"What's that awful stink?" It was O'Hara. He saw the paper spread out, the headline. He said, "Incredible, isn't it?"

"I could have predicted it," said Morris. He was shak-ing his head from side to side, but he was smiling.

O'Hara invited Morris over for a meal the next night. He said, "And don't forget to bring the wife! *She's* the one I want to chew the fat with."

Remembering Lil, Morris folded the paper and started down the corridor. He was stopped by Charlie Shankland (Latin America). Shankland said, "I'm sorry about this," meaning the invasion, and invited the Rosetrees for Saturday.

Lil cried that afternoon. She saw the paper and said, "Brave, brave people," and "My poor country, always trouble." At the O'Haras' and the Shanklands' Lil was asked about the Russians: how did she feel about them? what would she do if she were in Prague today? who would she support?

"You do not know how . . . messianic . . . are the Russians," she said. Morris had never heard her use that word before. He was pleased. "My husband," she went on, looking at Charlie and lowering her eyes, "My husband thinks they are okay, like you all do. But we know they are terrible—" She could not finish.

She had said "sinks" instead of "thinks." Morris was angry with himself for having noticed that. He wanted her to say more; he was proud and felt warm toward her. He was asked questions. Twice he replied, "Well, my wife says she thinks," ending each time "Isn't that right, Lil?" And each time Lil looked at him and bowed her head sadly in agreement.

Morris dug out his dissertation and read it, and threw half of it away. He made notes for new chapters and began consulting Lil, asking detailed questions and not interrupting her answers. He gave a lecture for the Political Science Club, and he was invited to Chicago to present a paper at a forum on the worsening situation in Czechoslovakia. He started buying an evening paper; he read of more students defying soldiers and scrawling Dubcek's name on the street with chalk. He followed the funeral of the boy who was shot, and he saw the Czechs, whom he often felt were *his* Czechs, beaten into silence by the Russians. But the silence did not mean assent; even less, approval. It was resistance. He knew them, better than most people knew them. Time had passed, but it was not very long after the first Russian tank appeared in Prague that Morris Rosetree came home from a lecture and whispered to his wife, "Lepska, I love you."

SINNING WITH ANNIE

MAKE NO MISTAKE ABOUT IT, I, ARTHUR VISWALINGAM, was married in every sense of the word, and seldom during those first years did I have the slightest compunction. Acceptance is an Asiatic disease; you may consider me one of the afflicted many. I was precisely thirteen, still mottled with pimply blotches, pausing as I was on that unhealthy threshold between puberty and adolescence. Annie (Ananda) was a smooth eleven, as cool and unripe as the mango old Mrs. Pushpam brings me each morning on a plate when I sit down to my writing. (Is it this green fruit before me now that makes me pause in my jolly memoir to take up this distressing subject, one that for so long has troubled my dreams and made my prayers pitiful with moans of penitential shame?) It was a long time before the eruptions of adolescence showed with any ludicrous certainty (I almost said absurtainty!) on Annie's face. I imagine it was around our third anniversary, the one we celebrated at the home of that oaf Ratnam, my cousin (his mother, another yahoo, unmercifully repeated a jape about our childlessness: "Perhaps they are not *doing* it right!"). I cannot be sure exactly when Annie became a woman: she always seemed to be a small girl

35

playing at being grown-up, worrying the cook and sweeper with her pouts, dressing in outlandish styles of sari, crying often and miserably—all of this, while we were married, an irritating interruption of my algebra homework.

At my present age I am certain of very little; I only know that I can no longer expect God to listen to my incessant wailing, and so I turn to my fellow man, not for indulgence but simply to give God a rest. This is the wet season in Delhi; the temple monkeys are drenched: they sit mournfully under the crassly painted arches, their fur sticking out in wet prickles, their pale blue flesh chilled with the monsoon, giving them the deathly look of the gibbons that turn up now and again, bloated and drowned in the open drains of this city. My pen spatters ink; I write slowly on unbleached foolscap with many half-starts and crossings-out. I can hear the wheezing of wind through the little midden of Asiatic rubbish that has accumulated in my lungs; I can feel my heart stretching and straining with each pump, like an old toad squatting in the basket of my ribs. To misquote the celebrated poet from Missouri, I am an old man in a wet month.

But imagine me, if you can, seventy years ago, standing on spindly legs (I thought all the world stood on spindly legs until I saw English shopgirls)—as I was saying, standing on spindly legs at the temple entrance, in my pint-sized turban, my hands clasped against my thirteen-year-old breast. All manner of hooting and shrieking from the street echoed in the temple: bargains being struck, coins and brown rupees exchanged for flesh and fruit. That was long ago; it has taken all this time for me to see the irony of those beastly hawkers.

Little imbecile that I was, I had no idea I was being swapped. I did not know that Annie's father had promised five thousand rupees to my father if the marriage transpired as arranged. Chits and promises had been exchanged; my parents had haggled while I played dawdling puddle games and kicked my football. And little did I know of my father's bankruptcy, my mother's idle, spendthrift ways; no, it pleased me that my father always seemed to be on holiday, my mother dressed richly in excellent shawls. How was I to know my father was lazy, my mother foolish; or, indeed, that I would have to pay for their sins with my chaste flesh?

We lived in princely fashion, with leisure and comfort that for all I know even a prince would envy: the lower class's idea of the voluptuous is always grander than the prince's, because it is unattainable. Their demons and gods, about which I shall speak presently, show them to be a very imaginative lot; coupled with their idleness this breeds a grotesquery all its own. My father's credit remained solid; had my father declared himself bankrupt very early on, or had my mother gone about in the market in tattered sari and worn sandals, a splintery wooden comb stuck in her hair instead of the ivory one she habitually wore, the final reckoning would have, I am convinced, come sooner. The people in our village were quite ignorant and easily gulled. Foolishness was a plague which descended on us early and stayed, not killing, but maiming: cripples abounded. In evidence of this, which I am sure my parents took careful note of, the villagers worshiped a whole zoo of beasts, a pseudospiritual menagerie: snakes, monkeys, elephants, goddesses with six arms and dreadful snouts, gods with elephantine ears, tusks and even wrinkled trunks. To be human was a crime against everyone; it was grotesque. Have I mentioned the cows? It pains me to recall the bovine benedictions I performed: I have stroked the hindquarters of a plaster cow until the paint flaked off and the stone itself was worn smooth—nay, made indentations in the plaster flanks with my praying fingers! I donged bells and keened, lit tapers, strewed petals. We Hindus have a curious faith that, in a manner of speaking, transforms a farmyard into a place of worship—a backward, rat- and snake-infested farmyard at that. The more dumb and stupid the idol, the more devoutly we pray. Mrs. Pushpam, for example, is at this moment with a hundred other yelping women, beating her tambourine before a smudged mezzotint of Shiva in a squalid bazaar. It should surprise no one to learn that two of the dozen or so words which English takes from my language are *goon* and *thug*; I would not be amazed, further, if *fanatic* and *dunderhead* had Sanskrit roots.

Where was I? Yes, at the temple. I was there because my father's credit had run out at last. No one else knew this of course: the bluff was still working. I think of a card game, symbol of bluff. I have never seen a child's face on a pack of cards, though I have in my mind a special pack, my father's, the cards marked Foolishness, Pomp, Ego, Greed, Idleness, Boastfulness; there is a face card as well: the painted image of a sallow prince, dressed ludicrously in finery, the little demented face staring with big eyes. It was this card my father played in the spring of 1898 (it was a "marrying year," as they say in my language) in the Laxshminarayan Temple, when he was released from his years of bluff, and I was bound up irrevocably with sin.

The Savior of the faith I embraced only this year similarly stood in a temple; he spoke wise words to his elders about Work, Duty and His Father's Business. The comparison with me is crude and unworthy, but it serves to throw my sin into bold relief. I too stood in an Eastern temple, but less confidently than the Nazarene; I stood with sweating elders and uttered inanities (God help me, I have already said something of my father's "business"!), stroked for the umpteenth time the cow's behind, the monkey's flank, mooed and crowed, in a tongue I would very willingly now like to disremember, the shrill syllables of my pagan faith, trumpeted like Ganpati, the elephant god, chattered like Hanuman, and let myself be anointed (under the circumstances, a sacrilegious verb) with unguents, perfumes, juices, nectars, spots of dust, rare oils and essences and—it shames me to mention this, though I promised to be ingenuous—devoured a reeking pudding made up of the excrement, dung I should say, of all the above-mentioned animals. Meanwhile a medium went into a trance and, eyeballs rolled up, scraped his tongue with a rusty sword after which he wrote asinine charms on yellow slips of paper with the blood. Talk about barbarism! You have no idea.

My bride, the child Annie, was heavily veiled, clothed with blossoms, orchids, a paraphernalia of frangipani and jacaranda, anything the idlers who arranged the wedding could lay their hands on. She was so small she could have been a corsage; and she was as mobile as Birnam wood. None of it meant much to me, neither the incantations nor the odors, the clanging temple nor the avaricious side glances of my "elders." My attention was fixed elsewhere: in the corner of the temple a beggarly snake charmer on his haunches blew a swollen flute, coaxing a sleek, swaying cobra out of a basket.

Picture our wedding night: two children entering an empty house, a small boy with dripping sweets clasped in one hand and, in the other hand, a sequined turban crammed with stale flower petals and old rupees; a small girl, head down, follows closely behind, clutching flowers, shuffling in gilt slippers that clack on the stone floor. The children are moving cautiously: both are afraid of the dark.

Our house was an extension to my father's. Annie and I had six rooms, though for that first year we lived in one; as children, even though the house was ours, we felt we were not entitled to more than that. In every way except one did we behave as children: we needed our parents' permission to buy sweets; we were not allowed to go to plays or to music shows alone; all our clothes and all my schoolbooks were bought by my father (we had not one piece to call our own); Annie, though my wife, never cooked, sewed or scrubbed; there were times when we were not allowed to dress ourselves. I can remember several occasions when we were tucked into bed (consider the implications of that phrase!). Thrice I was birched by my father in the presence of my wife.

Bear all this in mind as you read on. But before I begin, let me say that I have noticed in Western countries a certain evidence of urges before there is action on the part of the very young. Theirs, those gay souls, is a constant rehearsal of marital obligation long before the deed is done, a relatively harmless form of physical foolery, touching at private parts, playing Mommy and Daddy, dressing up like the oldsters do. This goes on manifesting itself in various forms up to the age of eighteen or twenty when, quite understandably, they are allowed the privacy and license to, as it were, get on with it.

In my savage country things are different, to say the least. While in the West you have, during this exploratory period, adults always within earshot, in our case (I should say village), for all practical purposes, we had none. Unlike the little chappies frolicking and dabbing at each other in English country gardens, our experience was painfully real and immediate, unrelieved by sport or jest. Sex, in marriage, loses much of its heartiness. I suppose our parents thought that one of the many semibeasts we went about worshiping would swoop down and rescue us at the crucial moment. To be frank, I haven't the slightest idea of what goes on in the Asian mind.

That first night was fairly typical of the ones that followed. There were so many. I led the way into the room; inside, Annie crept into a corner. Suspecting that I had lost her, I lighted a taper and slammed the door. She jumped, startled; I spied her crouching near a little altar. I wanted very much to talk to her, but could think of nothing to say except "Where do you live?" and I refrained from asking that; her reply would have been a polite, "Here, my husband." I offered her a sweet, one of our large vulgar *gulabjam*, made of paste and broken milk and covered with sugary syrup. She took it and ate it noisily, licking her fingers with her cat's tongue.

There was a screen in the room, a wicker frame with silk stretched across it and decorated with clumsy flowers: more of our degraded culture. When my sweets were gone I stuffed my money-filled turban under my pillow and went behind the screen to change into my pajamas. This done, I blew out the candle and crept into bed, ignoring my wife. It was not until I rolled over and shut my eyes that I heard the rustle of Annie's clothes. I could tell what she was taking off from the sounds each garment made when it was fumbled with: there was first the flutter of the withered flower strands as they were lifted over her head, the lisp of silk unwinding, and the hush of her stepping out of her petticoat; the thump and tinkle as she pulled her slippers off, the heel click as they were placed side by side at the foot of the bed; a tiny noise, the slow zip of fingernails scraping on flesh, her thumbs in the waistband of her bloomers, pulling them down her legs. Then the *fee, fee, fee* of a comb being drawn through young and silky hair.

I find this description unbearably arousing! Was that really *me* in that bed? Alas, yes. I must go on. There were no more noises, not even the padding of her little feet as she crossed to her side of the bed. She slipped under the sheet (I felt the cool breath of the sheet ballooning air past me). At my age I could not be expected to have any idea of female nakedness: even as I listened to Annie removing her clothes I could not imagine what she looked like and, believe me, lying next to her in bed hadn't the foggiest idea what would happen next. I thought we might go quietly to sleep: I had eaten a sufficiency of sweets, slurped yogurt, gorged myself on rice and *dhal*; my head rang from the powerful incense of the ceremony. I shut my eyes tightly and tried to sleep, but this seemed to give me a bad case of insomnia. I was trying too hard. And then it came, against my will: a little animal, a nasty little beast like the sort we worshiped, awoke in me and made me very warm. Annie seemed to have something to do with it. The image came to me then (it persists even now) of the small girl's circus act: she waves her hand over the slumbering puppy and, with only this gesture, makes him rise on his haunches, his forepaws up, his jaws apart, begging, his tongue sagging juicily through his teeth. This is the only perception I keep from my youth, that sinful score of years. I keep it like a little shell plucked from the shores of my childhood, never thrown away: the little girl dancing innocently in naked grace around the puppy, the puppy rising from haunches to hind legs and leaping up, nipping at the little girl with sharp teeth, snarling— not a puppy, but that more bestial word, *dog*—and knocking the girl over roughly. The dog is on all fours, standing on her frail little newly budded breasts and barking insistently in quivering jerks. They are not playing, they are beyond that, and no one is watching; there is something fierce about the whole thing. Fierce, fumbling and unsatisfying. It was thus with Annie and me.

The next morning, when I awoke, I found a string tied to the underpart of the bedstead. I followed it out of the room and down to my parents' parlor where there were chairs. The string ended in a small silver bell. Annie must have been making the bed or something as I stared at the bell, for it tinkled (was she patting the covers?), reminding me of my lack of success, *ting-a-ling*.

* * *

There was no shame, only a temporary sense of defeat. You would say I was not man enough. We have no equivalent phrase in our language. How could we? With small folk leaping into bed, fully married, at the age of eleven and thirteen, could we possibly have any sane concept of maturity? I am not a sociologist; I am a tired old man, an ashamed and angry tired old man, but I know that this is a different kettle of fish from what you are used to. You never saw anyone so young bunged into marriage as I was.

In a phrase you have it: a nation of children. It is cruel, but exceedingly accurate. If I was not a child, why should I leap on my bride of one day and bark like a dog, sniff her, butt her with my head, squeeze her until she cried out? Mind you, I squeezed her ankles, I squeezed her wrists: I did not know any better. Half my body had swollen in an unfamiliar manner and I was looking for a place to put it, to fit it in, a socket which I imagined was hidden somewhere on her pathetic little body. She lay; when I touched her roughly she squealed, but I must say that she did all she could. She tried her level best. I nuzzled, bit, screwed up my face and whined piteously into her cheek, all to no avail. If I may say so, it made matters somewhat worse, for nothing is so inflammatory to lust as delay. I burned. I married *and* burned. This went on for many months.

At the same time I was at school, preoccupied with the trivia that besets the schoolboy. My education, in light of the bizarre circumstances of my private life, pained me as often as it gave me release. How I envied the simple lives of those characters we read about, Oliver Twist whose only problem was to find a way of coping with those rogues and ruffians, all the others oiling their cricket bats, having tea and buttered scones in well-appointed parlors, throwing their hats in the air at rugger matches. All so jolly next to what I had to face! Naturally I could explain none of this to my wife. Our marriage was now a year old (I was in Form Two), and we spent our time sitting dumbly in our house or picking flowers for festivals, always avoiding the subject that seemed to turn the sharp Indian sunlight into deep gloom. I cannot say I dreaded going to bed; I will say that I viewed the whole affair with some little apprehension. My desire to succeed befogged my mind and made me less capable of success.

Inevitably of course we did succeed; I will not trouble you with details which, in their entirety, do not make a very pretty parcel; my gift for expression begins to lurch some distance this side of stark nakedness. It would be an error to venture nearer than I have already. What intrigued me during this time was that once I had succeeded I could not understand why I had ever failed. This success marked the onset of school latenesses that very nearly ended in my expulsion, my failure to complete the most rudimentary homework or, in brief, any task that was performed outside the confines of our wretched little bedroom. I puffed and panted (we are not a hardy race, in spite of what the rabble of nationalists may assert when speaking with a rank foreigner: never trust an Asiatic); my lust knew no bounds, yet there was a limit to my competence, of that I am shamefully aware, doubly so as I write this.

I should now very much like to say a thing or two about my sin, namely lust. This sin is commonly, and not altogether mistakenly, classed with gluttony, envy and the other four deadly sins. Alcoholism, a manifestation of gluttony, may serve as a preliminary comparison: one sees drunken louts shambling about the streets searching for a drink shop. Their behavior is unseemly. But lust is worse; it is in a class all its own, for it afflicts man in a more acute way than does the craving for spirits. Besides being a most private degradation, gluttony for drink lacks a certain urgency which is essential to any definition of lust. Thirst, sometimes associated with lust, should not be at all; thirst is a sense of wanting, together with the slimy accumulation on the mouth, tongue and throat of a layer of bubbly but not juicy saliva that wants slaking. It comes in stages, the swelling tongue, the parching throat beginning to build up that slimy coat, and then the urge. Lust, on the other hand, *is* urge, a fullness that is in actual fact closer to anger than to gluttony: a fit of full feverish temper which puts the blood immediately on the boil, causes muscles to tense and harden with something approaching criminal determination and starts a warm diabolical rosiness to effervesce throughout one's limbs, drenching the body in one's own sweat like a sputtering joint of basted beef. You readers who are not lustful but who may have quick tempers may usefully compare your tantrums with reechy passion; even the descriptive vocabulary remains somewhat constant: one is aroused quickly to both anger and lust; one grows excessively hot with both, loses one's reason and turns beefy red. The emotions of lust and anger proceed with equal speed, which is to say they are frantically brief when given the most liberty, and longest in duration (and more intense) when an attempt is made to curb or conceal them. The difference is this: one may take out one's wrath on the leg of a table, but lust is only satisfied by the leg of a strumpet. It is possible to allay one's angry feelings in private; lust involves other people and I believe because it does so, is the greater corruption. It takes two, as the saying has it, to do the tango. Having said that, I shall say no more about it.

Annie changed. No longer the hard coil of dark wires I had married, but indolent and alluring, and yet remarkably compact, like those bready sweets we in Asia addict ourselves to and canker out teeth with. Her cheeks grew plump, her budding breasts swelled into two tingling and pipped morsels of fruit, and indeed all her flesh took on a sleepy thickness which I took the devil's own delight in pinching in this wise: extending my claw, I would grasp a bit of her flesh between my thumb and forefinger and give a sharp tweak, pretending all the while that I had scooped a collop of meat from, say, her cheek or belly; and then I would pretend to eat it. I realize now that had she grown ugly I might have ceased sinning and taken my solemn vow of celibacy much sooner. But she grew ever more attractive, which goes to show that the devil may take many forms, even that of grace and beauty, provided that it is dark enough to conceal his cloven hoof: where lust is concerned, darkness is just around the corner. Far from being horrible, the object of our lust may appear virginal; the sin itself, to the wanton child with the corrupt parents, seems incredibly delicious on first taste.

Prying old Pushpam has returned from her fatuous orgy of monkey worship. I must be quick; the hag is snorting

and fretting in the hallway, wondering which vegetables
to stew. And just as well; I should say no more about
sinning with Annie and its attendant sorrows. There were
times when I wanted to be done with the whole business:
my penitent trembling transformed me from hermit to nut
case, and brutality welling within me sloshed up past my
gizzard to splash at the back of my eyes. With my prayers
wobbling every which way like bats in my closed room,
and pleas squeaking past my numb lips, I felt the urge to
punish: I was at the Delhi Gate when the British returned;
I led them to the flea pots and flesh pits, the drink shops
and temples and, in a bloody crusade, we crushed the life
out of the verminous population. This accomplished, we
peopled the country anew, cleanly, without mess, with
colder holy folk from frozen places. Those times, had
Annie walked through the door, as Mrs. P. had just done,
I would have put my pen down, risen and wrapped my
still-nimble fingers around her neck to throttle the life out
of her. Taking into account the extent of my sin and general misery, that action must seem to you totally justifi-
able. I cannot say. Latterly, I get fewer and fewer of these
brutal urges. No, I doubt that I would do that now, I very
much doubt it. You will call me silly, but most likely I
would fumble out of my chair and screech across the
carpet, sleeves and cuffs billowing, sandals aflap; and,
pity me deeply, I would fall before her and touch my lips
to her instep as if she were the Queen of Heaven.

A LOVE KNOT

ON RAINY NIGHTS IN THAT PART OF BOSTON, THE Charles Street area, antique gas lamps lighted the narrow side streets which were swollen with a paving of cobblestones. Like the lamps, the stones had been left intact, and they were so carefully preserved in a way that caused such inconvenience that the nostalgia they represented was vulgar, an obnoxious pride. There was no love in it. It is that way with keeping old things: they are flaunted and handled and gaped at. Collectors and conservers are arrogant; many Bostonians are that way, and several I knew flinched when I told them how I had once seen my cousin tear the brass guts out of an expensive Victorian oil lamp and solder in a light socket. He thought it looked better with a plastic flex trailing from a hole he punched in its base. My cousin should have seen those gas lamps in Boston. Their clean windows framed small bags of white light and made the cobblestones gleam like glazed loaf tops.

With the love knot in my pocket Walnut Street was my destination, but all those streets had the same effect on me: turning into one from the traffic and honkings of busy Charles, I began to walk more slowly, as if I had been hurried back a hundred years and cooled on the way. I didn't see the nostalgia as arrogance: the discovery of this oldness was private and all my own, not urged on me by an anxious host. Because I was young and a stranger and because my first experience of that city had been vicarious in the most distancing way—through reading about it in novels—I wished to prolong these sensations of the age I understood, the city of quaintness and crime. By slowing down and remembering, I exhumed in my memory a grateful reverence for the solidness and the apparent calm, and hoped that the feeling would remain at least until I reached that crusted hydrant or that angular leaning house with the mullioned windows at the corner. I strained to hear the hoofbeats and creaking leather of a gasping horse, the wobbling clatter of carriage wheels approaching, or the man in the black opera cape tapping his cane toward a doorway draped in fog boas. I saw no one's face and I sensed that behind the brick walls of houses lay intrigue's moist dread and expectancy: a shadowy drawing room, chairs arrayed facing each other like old aunts who refuse to die, a cold fire, untouched sandwiches curling on the edges of a plate, a mantelpiece clock set in porcelain, an odor of foreign tobacco, a male corpse lying in a posture of frozen hilarity, some blood running into the pile of an expensive carpet—all the props in the literary stage set of a finished murder.

I was a student then, and on an errand, and if I made a great deal of the atmosphere it was because I had recently arrived from the worst city in the world, my birthplace, Calcutta—not, as I was often forced to explain to Americans, a fancifully named town in a Midwestern state, but the real place, in Bengal. Having left Calcutta I knew I would never go back, though I was bonded to the Government of West Bengal and I had promised that on my return I would work at a low salary for five years in the civil service to repay the loan that had been given to me. I am not a liar by nature; it hurt me to make the promise of returning after I earned my degree. But my family no longer exists for me: most are dead, and those who are not dead I never knew well. It was my plan to flee. The university in the Boston suburb was also part of my plan—I would not have gone anywhere else.

The idea of crime in those parts was not wholly literary remembrance of Bostonians with swords sheathed in walking sticks or genteel poisonings (strychnine has the sound and feel of a long, sharp knife—the sword-cane and the poisoning are linked in my imagination). All this was ten years ago, a time when so many women, most of them elderly, were sexually outraged and then strangled—I may have reversed the order here—by a lunatic handyman. On my first visit to Walnut Street a daily newspaper displayed in a steel rack in front of a drugstore had the alarming headline FEAR STALKS THE HILL. Idling foreigners were reported to the police, and I expected to be stopped and subjected to a frisking and made to explain my errand. I was a total stranger in that place. Although my mother was a white American and my father a German, my passport was Indian and so is my accent still: I speak with my lips pursed and subtly transpose the first letters of the words *very well*. I had always been taught to think of myself as an Indian, more particularly Bengali, for in addition to being born near Calcutta, I lived there until the age of twenty-one, at which time I received my bursary. In Boston at the time of these stranglings, I felt that I, an Indian, was conspicuous. I was surprised that no one took the slightest notice of me. In coffee shops and, occasionally, buying subway tokens, I was asked to repeat myself; the requests were extremely polite. But in large cities speech is seldom necessary, and when it is used it is functional phrase-book language; except for the few times when I was asked to repeat what I said, a number or the name of a subway station, my accent went unnoticed. My color, of course, blended perfectly. At that time the word *colored* was still used to describe black people. I was not taken for, though I felt, colored.

My background was of interest to the girls I dated, and the information that I had resolved to suppress I found myself elaborating upon, as soon as I saw that it caused no discomfort to the listener. I am not a gregarious person and these petty details of my life were a relief from small talk. It soon reached the point where if I was not asked, I offered, saying, "Did you know that I'm an Indian?" which never failed to produce the question, "You mean an *Indian* Indian or the other kind?" I was envied for my origins but I selected, leaving many details unspoken, for I had once dwelt on some squalid aspects of my upbringing with a girl I especially liked, thinking of ways to interest her and casting about in my memory for impressive sorrows and hardships, and I was so absorbed in this that it was some time before I looked up and saw that I was making her cry.

The love knot, in gold, I found among my mother's possessions after she died, of an illness diagnosed as cerebral malaria, in our house in Calcutta in 1957. It was in an envelope sealed on the flap with red wax, a buff-paper envelope, much thumbed and furry with use, bearing on the front an address in my mother's handwriting, *To*: *George Chowdree, 22 Walnut Street, Boston, Massachusetts*. It was with three bangles, an out-of-date passport, my birth certificate and some things of my father's (his spectacles, some old coins, green-brown paper money, his copy of the *Ramayana* in a German translation), items of no value. He had died years before, alone my mother said, in another city in India. The sealed envelope had been addressed a very long time ago, and it looked as if it had been carried around, for the corners were tearing and the wrinkles and bulges in the envelope were a shadowy pattern the shape of the small object inside. It could not be mailed. I opened it, for these reasons and also because I was curious. There was no note inside, only the love knot, worked in the most delicate filigree perhaps by one of our Bengali goldsmiths. That the name was George Chowdree amused me. He was obviously a Christian Indian, one of a group my mother detested: she spat at the sight of a black priest and she said that if I ever entered a Catholic church she would kill me. This anger in her was rare. She was a peaceful soul, and she was a very devout Hindu.

I am, I suppose, a Hindu myself. My interest in the name George Chowdree lay in the fact that its pattern was nearly my own name in reverse: my first name is Hindu and my surname European. Danny, as I'm called, is given as Daneeda on my passport; my surname, Schum, which is German, rhymed with zoom in India and now, in America, it rhymes with thumb. Persons of mixed identity like me find it simpler to agree with the stranger's assessment. I am what other people take me for; I never challenge their assumptions. When they say, "I guess your father went to India during the war," I say he did. They are probably right. I never knew my father, and the little I know of my background is enough to prevent me from wondering further. It was my mother who raised me, her only child; she took me to the temple, she enrolled me in school and stitched and mended my uniforms, she encouraged me to get a job in the civil service, she tried to keep me innocent. While she was certainly puritanical, she had developed the Indian habit of going to the movies on Saturday afternoons; it was her one recreation, and I shared it purely to please her. The films were extremely boring, their plots predictable and melodramatic (defiant lovers, feuding families, women dying in childbirth), but the songs—a dozen or so in each movie—were pleasant. My mother hummed them as she cooked, crouching next to a smoky fire and stirring and slapping dough cakes and turning from the smoke to sigh and push her hair—which was light brown—out of her eyes. I know now that my mother was a very beautiful woman; it is something that one discovers late—it may even be the mark of manhood to see one's mother as a woman who was once beautiful. As an orthodox Hindu, my mother never wore jewelry; her only ornament was a vermilion caste mark, the shape of a narrow candle flame, on her very white forehead. It surprised me that she had owned a love knot.

But there it was, after her cremation, in my hand. I slipped it into a clean envelope and wrote out the address of George Chowdree, and for weeks afterward I repeated the address to myself. I took the same comfortable refuge in it that one does in an incantation. Studying for my Higher School Certificate, I copied this address on the flyleaf of my volume of *The Secret Agent*, which was one of the set books in English that year and which, now that I think of it, may have provided some of the London atmosphere that I later associated with that area of Boston: Verloc could have managed his seedy shop on Charles Street, and Winnie's carriage bumped over cobblestones just like those I saw on Walnut. I made one alteration in the address. Instead of Chowdree's name, I wrote, with the yearning one feels in the solitude of early youth, my own name, and under it *Walnut Street* and the city. For as long as I could remember I had wanted to escape from India, and now I had a place to escape to. It might have been the reason I did so well in my examinations.

In my mind I saw a street in America lined with walnut trees; there was only one house on the street that I could see clearly, the others were smaller and much blurred. Number twenty-two was a cheerful house, freshly painted, and it resembled a colonnaded house in Calcutta I was fond of walking past, an elegant but deserted one, where an Englishman had once lived. My scholarship went through after some delays; I was given a folder of directions and authorizations, printed on villainous paper; and I sailed from Madras.

I did not go to Walnut Street immediately. I wanted to discover the place slowly, as one does a painting in a museum, approaching it from a great distance and picking out details as one draws nearer for the close, final dazzle. I bought a map; I studied that. I walked in other parts of the city, where the docks are, where the insurance companies are, the bookstores, the Irish bars with old photographs of bare-fisted boxers in the windows, along the river near the hospitals, the Chinese district of four streets bordered by strip clubs and a large school of dentistry. And when I had explored the peripheries of the Charles Street area, noticing on the way a gloomy building housing the Theosophical Society, many antique shops and boarding houses (the doors ajar, pay phones on the wall), I walked to the corner of Beacon and Charles and then down Charles, pausing often, to Walnut, where I first saw that newspaper headline. I examined my map one last time. It was late on a rainy afternoon in August and I shielded the map in my hand as I looked from it to the street sign and then down the sidewalk. People walked quickly past me in the warm drizzle with their heads down, holding bright umbrellas or, if they had no umbrellas, making visors over their eyes with their hands. I was splashed by a car just before I turned into Walnut; but this was not the street I expected. The antique gas lamps were lighted, and so were most of the cobbles beneath them, glazed individually in pools of illumination. But the rest was dark, and there were few trees, all with wet, heavy green leaves, planted in holes in the sidewalk and protected by cylindrical wooden fences. The houses were all three-storied, most of them joined, with narrow plots of grass at the fronts. The even numbers were on the opposite side of the street. I went cautiously and found number twenty-two, watched for a moment, then walked around the block to a coffee shop where I had a sandwich and tea. The darkness outside was false, caused by the storm; I wanted night, and I walked until it enclosed the city. I went back to Walnut Street again, and passing the house, I saw through the lighted front window a girl's face, laughing at someone I could not see, and the face of the girl was as dark as all those I had left in Calcutta.

That was strange. I had prepared myself for a man's face, and, even more, for a particular man, one I had seen in a Bengali film, a plump-necked actor who always played the role of a businessman, a frequent traveler, a man of some importance; I had superimposed this important actor's face on George Chowdree. He was my stereotype—healthy Indians traveled, skinny ones stayed at home. Here I betray the theatrical side of my plan. It was melodrama, worthy of the Indian film which is filled with such paraphernalia: my dead mother's piece of ornate jewelry always in my pocket, my cleverly obtained scholarship, my search, my wanderings about the city—striking poses as if I was being watched. And soon I fitted that dark girl's face into this melodrama, as more appropriate then the man's I expected.

It was not my purpose to knock on the door and introduce myself. The busy strangler made everyone suspicious, doors were closed to strangers; it was not even a time for casual visiting, for people were no less anxious on an unfamiliar sidewalk than they were in their own houses, and footsteps behind one took on the jarring insistence of summoning nighttime knocks on a door.

I saw the girl's face; I was satisfied; I went away. For many days I called the laughing face to mind, the street, the lighted window, until all the anticipated details of my previous fantasy had been replaced by the actual details—

unanticipated but now appropriate—of what I saw that evening. It was still fantasy, but substantiated by enough reality to make me patient in my errand. Something of my patience, deliberately exercised to sustain my little drama, may be seen when I say that I did not look up Chowdree's name in the telephone directory until after I visited the house. I could have done this as soon as I landed in America. I did not. And finally, when I did, it was as I expected, the only one in the book, at the right address. But to my surprise his initials were followed by the abbreviation for medical doctor.

For minutes I searched for credible symptoms, envisaging an allusive chat with Chowdree the physician as he tapped my back and crushed the wooden tongue depresser into his wastebasket. I could become his patient. I rejected this as too convenient and, as I had by now become acquainted with American medical charges, too expensive. I think I might have tried it, but after I saw that girl's face I knew my approach would be through her. She was about my own age; she was pretty, probably a student like me and, quite black, was me in negative. It was a symmetry I enjoyed. While I thought about this I fancied that the shadow I cast in that late summer reverie was like this girl, dark and altering in rippling angles as I walked on uneven ground, a foreshortened reflection of my own personality, changeable and intriguing, joined at my foot sole.

I did what the solitary person or the lonely lover often does. He knows that it is morbid to sit in his room and chew on his misery; he goes out and, at the slightest suggestion, he follows women, marking them in buses or in stores and then trailing after them, keeping at a safe undetectable distance and relentlessly keeping them in sight, so that their resolution—those quick woman's steps—becomes this, promising fulfillment. Women march more hectically than men and as they approach their destination they become positively frantic because women do not watch their feet or swing their arms, and when they speed up they acquire a mechanical bustle, and nearly always their calves stand out in smooth oblongs and the backs of their ankles become hard and pinched. A foreigner in a city watches other people; he tries to imitate their rhythm so he studies their movements. The reason I assigned for the women's speeding up was that unlike men they never glanced around as they walked and I decided that this provoked uneasiness and, consequently, a nervous speed.

So it was with this dark girl. She attended a school of fine arts that was housed in an old building on Marlborough Street; I had followed her to the place and later wrote a letter asking whether I might do a part-time course with them. The fees were out of the question. I continued to follow the girl to other likely spots. She used the Boston Public Library twice a week, the section devoted to Oriental art. I applied for a borrower's card and began studying there myself twice a week at the little tables adjacent to the ones she used. When she entered a stack, I entered a parallel one and, pretending to read, peered at her back. One day I saw her take a book; the subject was Indian miniatures of the Mogul period. She used it for the afternoon. I stayed at my desk, watching. After she was gone I looked on the shelf and saw that it was not there. She had checked it out.

A month later, on a day when normally she did not use the library, I looked for the book. It was not on the shelf. I looked it up in the card catalogue and noted down the author's name, and then I requested it at the main desk. The white-haired lady there wore spectacles hung on a chain around her neck. I showed her the card and asked when the book was due to be returned. Spectacles were put on, drawers pulled out, index cards flipped and thumbed. The book had not been borrowed, said the lady, and was I absolutely sure it was not on the shelf? She repeated the call number. I said no. She said, rising, that it may have been put on another shelf.

We searched; she for a long time, I for only a few minutes. I knew then the book had been stolen.

And I knew the thief! A discovery! I had found her laughing and recorded her way of walking; I knew her subject and her school and many of her habits. These were obvious things. Now I had discovered a weakness, a deep secret. Many husbands would have trouble discovering this in their wives, but I was more patient than any husband, and more persistent than most lovers. I fantasized the kind of device necessary for such a theft: a sling, a pocket hung between her thighs on straps attached to a belt, the whole business hidden by her long skirt. (I knew her complete wardrobe and the ways she varied it, though once she surprised me with a new silk scarf.)

Her long skirts were out of fashion, but her face was so pretty that in clothes cut the wrong length, and so plain and featureless, she seemed to be anticipating a bold fashion. Her face was the same shade as her arms, deeply colored, with a high dark polish, the gloss of the race, a prominent nose balanced above by a strong forehead and brow, and below by full brown lips. She was Bengali, there was no doubt of that; the face, the thick black hair told it, the warm melancholy of her large eyes, the thin arms and sharp elbows, the long fingers, busy with mischief and pencils, nacreous fingernails, her air of independence, walking so swiftly, her responsible innocence concealing her crime.

I had followed her for months, through Boston streets, in department stores, stood with my back to her and watched her reflection in the window of a travel agency as she walked like a ghost through the sign *Puerto Rico $49*, as she browsed among the sidewalk bins of a secondhand bookshop. Her movements were unchanging: I could meet her bus, join her discreetly at the Hayes-Bickford for a coffee or follow her blindly, streets away, walking parallel on Boylston as she walked on Commonwealth Avenue, and I knew precisely when I could turn and allow our paths to cross. I was daring in the Main Reading Room of the library, sitting across the varnished table from her, memorizing her hands, for the lamps at eye level prevented her from seeing me. I kept maps of her movements; I could meet her head-on; I passed by her school and rehearsed conversations with her, and during her school's winter break, when her movements became slightly irregular (no school, more stores and library) I was half in love with her.

Her name was Dorothy Chowdree. I learned that early in December in the ridiculously painstaking way I had found out that she stole the book on Indian miniatures (and two others, also about Indian art). Now borrowing is done with numbers, but at that time the borrower wrote his name on two cards that were kept in a brown pocket glued to the inside back cover of the book; these cards were handed over when the book was taken out. I noted one book she had taken; it was returned on the date due; it bore her name. Simple. I noticed one other thing from my watching slot in Middle Eastern Art: there was a book she always used but never took out. It wasn't possible for her to steal this one; it was very large, with color plates, bound in full calf. Its subject was Indian ornaments and jewelry.

For several weeks in March I neither followed her nor used the library, and toward the beginning of April I picked up again and found her exactly where I knew she would be, at 4:30 on a Friday, walking away from her school to a cup of coffee at the Hayes-Bickford and then a two-hour session in the Oriental collection. I saw her disappear around the corner; I lingered at the school and then went in. Some students, long-haired girls with green book bags and bulging portfolios were clomping down a wooden, spiral staircase. They paused at a bulletin board, read, and passed by me. I had a look at the bulletin board myself: a tea was announced ("Pourer, B. Yardley"), a lecture at a museum, a summer school in Vermont. Dorothy's name was given twice, as organizer of a dance at the Biltmore for the Spring Weekend ("Single, $3.50") and as chairman of a lecture on Mondrian. The lecture was in a week's time, the dance in mid-May. Savoring the pure pleasure of expectation, I decided on the dance.

The weather grew mild; it still rained often, but the rain did not dry so quickly on the streets as it had done in the winter freeze. Streets, grass and sidewalks stayed wet, and in the early evenings and at night there were reflections on Walnut Street, reminding me of my first day, when I discovered that house and Dorothy's face in the lighted window. I was less patient now, for I had decided that Dorothy's industry at the library must mean that she was in her last year at the school. It would not be easy to trace her after her graduation. All my energies went into planning for the dance. I ferreted out a student from my college who knew where tickets could be bought for the Spring Weekend dance at the Biltmore. I borrowed

money, bought a dark suit and a new tie and had my shoes
resoled. Dorothy was also preparing for the dance: she
bought shoes and yards and yards of silk from an importer
just off Washington Street.

A week before the dance I entered the library early and
went to the Oriental section. Dorothy had not arrived. I
found the large leather volume on Indian ornaments and
slipped an envelope inside. It was a new envelope, addressed to Dorothy; inside was my mother's love knot. I
replaced the book on the shelf and took my usual place
at Middle Eastern Art. I could see a tweed coat moving
slowly through Dorothy's stack, fingering the spines. A
man's ringed hand took a book from the shelf, opened it
to the flyleaf, put it back. He then sidled toward the Indian
ornaments book and, just as quickly, stepped away. Dorothy was beside him, her shoes clicking, heaving the book
down.

American bars are the darkest places imaginable. In the
Biltmore bar I had a whiskey and watched the students,
dressed for the dance, walking past the window of the
bar into the hotel lobby. I counted them so as to be sure
that the ballroom would be full when I arrived, and when
I had thirty-two couples I followed. Dorothy had not
passed the bar, but I knew that as organizer she must
have arrived early. I saw her as soon as I entered the
ballroom; she was not hard to miss.

She was wearing a sari, blue with a gold border and
not the shoes I had seen her buy but small embroidered
slippers with curling toes. Her dress was correct, the sort
that might be worn for an Indian festival or a wedding.
She wore bangles on both wrists and one on her left ankle
and when I saw her she was deep in conversation with
an elderly gentleman whom I took to be the president of
her school; he was bearded and wore a silk handkerchief
in his breast pocket. I remained in a corner, near a palm,
an intruder, and I saw, as I expected, that Dorothy was
wearing the love knot on a chain around her neck. I
squinted and made out a neatly painted caste mark on her
forehead, vermilion.

I do not know how to dance, and although I had prepared for the dance by deviously getting the ticket and

borrowing money for my clothes, I should have included a few dancing lessons, for I knew that I was going to talk to Dorothy this evening. The conversation I had practiced I imagined taking place as we were twirling around the room. But the band was playing loudly and I could see from the couples already on the floor that this dance step was beyond me. Half a dozen songs and an hour later I decided that unless the lights were lowered and the band was playing more slowly my plans would be ruined. A bad dancer can fake it if the music is slow and no one is watching. I went out of the ballroom and found a man in overalls and genially bribed him to dim the lights.

The first slow number was "Blue Moon." Dorothy danced with the elderly bearded gentleman. So she was a bad dancer, too! As she moved around the floor I edged over to where she had been standing; the music ended. There was clapping. She walked toward me. I smiled at her, an over-rehearsed grin that was nearly wild, but she returned it. I had to speak to her now.

I did so, but to this day I have no idea what happened to my tongue. I often think of this—I think of it as much as I do her face—and I still cannot understand it; there seems no explanation. I opened my mouth; my sentence was "I've been admiring your sari all evening," but I spoke it not in English but in Bengali.

Her eyes widened. I blushed and stared at the love knot, and I saw it as I had once done, in my hands in my mother's room in Calcutta.

"You speak Hindi," said Dorothy. An American accent in that beautiful Bengali mouth.

"No," I said in Bengali, and then, "No, not Hindi," I said in English, with my Indian accent. I was not doing well.

She wrinkled her nose.

"I have been admiring your sari all evening," I said, almost in panic. "But when I saw your jewel—it is a Bengali jewel, is it not?—I felt I had to speak in Bengali."

"Where did you learn it?" she asked, eager.

"A few lessons . . . private teacher . . ."

"Can you give me his name? I'm trying to learn—"

"He died," I said, and she made me regret my lie.

"Oh, I'm awfully sorry," she said, her face going sad.

"A long time ago," I added, and hearing "These Foolish Things" asked her to dance. My head was swimming.

She placed her hand on my shoulder; I embraced her and we were off, intimate as lovers. She said, "Some idiot put practically all the lights off. You can't see your hand in front of your face."

It was true. Perhaps I had given the man in overalls too much money. I said, "Oh, but I can see you wery vell."

She was humming the song in my ear.

"You must have lived in the States for a long time to pick up such a strong American accent. Not so?"

"I was born here," said Dorothy. "But my father was born in India, in Calcutta."

"Imagine that," I said. "And your mother?"

"Indian, too. But born in England. Kinda complicated, huh?"

"They met here?"

"In England," she said, "where my father was studying."

"Forgive my questions."

"That's okay. I have to explain this about once a week. As a matter of fact I was just saying the same thing to the dean. That's him over there with the beard, if you can see him in this spooky room."

"Odd," I said, "your father coming all this way. To America."

"Not so odd when you consider that his first wife was an American. But like they say, that was in another country."

I had no more questions. The dance ended. People were clapping.

But she was saying, "I can't understand why he came here. I'm leaving for India the day after tomorrow. I can hardly wait."

"Who knows," I said. "You might meet an Indian boy and marry him and never leave India."

"Not if my father has anything to do with it!" she said, and she raised her eyebrows and laughed loudly and I watched the love knot rising and falling at her throat, a jewel pulsing warmly on that dark velvet skin. She excused herself and disappeared, but I still saw the love knot, the gold threads of the filigree, meeting and crossing and meeting again. And I had a vision of a child I once saw in Calcutta, tracing figure eights in the dust with a wobbling stick. I watched and he drew a dozen or more, and the more he traced the more the figure changed, so that just before he left off, the final lines in each figure which had touched with such symmetry at the beginning ceased to meet at all and left a line curving at an angle in the dust, the open hourglass of an imperfect eight.

WHAT HAVE YOU DONE
TO OUR LEO?

▲▲▲▲▲▲▲▲▲▲▲▲▲▲▲▲▲▲▲▲▲▲▲▲▲▲▲▲▲▲▲

AT THE END OF THE MEAL, THE SUNDAY CURRY LUNCH which many of the expatriates in Dar es Salaam ate in the upstairs dining room of the Rex Hotel, Ernie Grigson leaned over and whispered seriously and slowly to Leo Mockler's ear: "I'm going to ask you for a big favor some time when I'm sober." Ernie found his glass and swallowed some beer. He added, "Mention it to me tomorrow, okay?"

Leo said yes, expelling it quickly with a vaporous belch, and as he did he saw Margo at the end of the table watching the two of them. Although Margo did not speak, she had the staring look of the practiced wife who knows without hearing him what her husband is saying.

But Ernie and Margo weren't married. They had planned to be months before, and then, out of the blue, Amy—Ernie's wife—went to India with the two children. Amy was living in an *ashram* outside Bombay. She wrote letters which were vague and dreamy and which always ended with demands for money. She never mentioned divorce. Ernie wondered if perhaps she was ill (the food? the heat?—Amy had never been strong). He wrote to the elderly Canadian lady who ran the *ashram;* he asked about

61

Amy. The lady wrote back in shaky script on handmade paper, stamped at the top with a Hindu symbol in blue: Amy was fine and the children were happy; "Amy's thoughts are serene and with us. She has many friends here. It will confuse her to preoccupy her mind with the separation. Amy needs time."

Ernie was angry: Amy in India had all the time in the world! And it had been understood that the divorce was a mutual wish. In those last months before Amy left for Bombay they had even stopped discussing the divorce: the arguments ended and the indifference that followed was more final than silence, worse than their quarreling had ever been.

Margo had moved in with Ernie the day Amy left. Leo visited them. He could sense their tension, which was lovers' tension, haphazardly pitching them into moods. Marriage, they agreed, was a trivial, nearly silly ceremony—but Ernie was still married to Amy and that mattered. Three times Leo heard the elderly Canadian lady's letter being read out; the last time it was read by Margo, who was pregnant now.

It was April in Dar es Salaam, and the rains were on them. The road to Ernie's house was sodden, and the raised sections at the edges broke off in chunks. There were a number of simple brown puddles which proved bottomless and swallowed the wheels of cars. And insects, seemingly given life by the floods of rainwater, crawled over the furniture and clung to windows. Even when it was not raining the air was heavy with wetness and insect racket. Ernie said that screens killed the breeze.

Leo, who lived at a boarding house, The Palms, a mile up the Oyster Bay Road, stopped driving all the way out to Ernie's. He saw the couple only on Sundays at the curry lunch. He was glad he did not see them often, because Margo's mood now did not concern the divorce anymore but was rather a tight shrewish incomprehension over why Ernie had married Amy in the first place. And Leo, once used as a witness, was expected to take sides. So it was "What do *you* think, Leo?" and also the rain that kept him away.

* * *

On Monday at five Leo pushed through the swinging saloon doors of the Rex and saw Ernie at the end of the bar, standing with one foot on the brass rail, studying the deeply scarred dart board.

"Large Tusker," said Leo to the barman, drawing beside Ernie and startling him.

"Rough day?" asked Ernie. He held his glass to his lips.

"The usual," said Leo. He worked at the National and Grindlays on Shirazi Street. He seldom spoke about his job to Ernie, who had something to do with traffic control at the airport, and thought naively (but like most other people) that Leo was rich because he worked in a bank. "I get long leave in September," said Leo. "I need it, too. I'm thinking of going back via Beirut and Athens."

"I might be able to do something for you—get you a concession, reduced rates, that sort of thing," said Ernie.

"Really?" Ernie had never made an offer like that before; and the most Leo had allowed Ernie at the bank was jumping the queue on Saturday mornings at the end of the month. "As a matter of fact I was also thinking of going to Prague, but it costs a bit extra."

"I could fix it for you," said Ernie. "There's a connecting flight to Prague from Athens. Have you booked?"

"No," said Leo.

"Write down the places you want to go on a piece of paper. Leave it to me. I'll take care of it."

Then Leo remembered what Ernie had said on Sunday. He was going to mention it. But it seemed so obvious: the favor in return.

"What are you drinking?" asked Leo.

"I'm all right," said Ernie. He looked into his glass and said, "You remember what I asked you yesterday?"

"The favor?"

"That's right," said Ernie, and tried to chuckle. "Well, the other day I was trying to think who was my best friend. I thought of Charlie and Agnes, Alan, the boys at the airport. And you know what? I couldn't think of one that I could rely on."

"Money?" asked Leo. He felt sure it was not, but said it to help Ernie along.

"No. I don't have much, but that's the thing, see? This is the one thing money won't buy."

"You've got me in suspense," said Leo.

"It's my divorce," said Ernie. He put his glass down, and with his hands empty he seemed to become conscious of their trembling. He picked them up and made fists and began to rub his eyes, speaking tiredly as he did so: "I've been seeing lawyers about it, and they all say it's hopeless. There are only two legal grounds for divorce here in Tanganyika." A long-time resident, Ernie always used the country's colonial name. "Nonconsummation and adultery, just like the U.K. And since I've got two kids I can't very well say I never poked my wife, can I?" He laughed briefly and took his fists from his eyes, which were now very red. "So that leaves me with adultery."

"It happens in the best of families," said Leo.

"Sure," said Ernie, "but did you ever think how hard it is to prove? The lawyers tell me that I have to supply the name of the chap and of course his address. Then I have to give the number of times and the places where I think it happened. If I can't give the details my divorce is up the spout." Ernie shook his head. "God, I haven't had a good night's sleep in ages."

"Amy's no help, I suppose."

"Useless," said Ernie. "Absolutely useless. I send a check every bloody month and she never thanks me. She's only written a couple of times. She wants a tape recorder, she wants a camera. I don't know what she *does* with the money—a hundred quid goes a long way in India." In a resigned tone Ernie said, "But she always took me for granted, you know."

"Well, who do you think it was that—" Leo stopped deliberately, but Ernie simply watched Leo's eyes and showed no inclination to speak. "That, um, committed adultery with her?"

"That's just it!" Ernie said. "She *didn't*. That's only the grounds."

"Oh, the grounds," said Leo. "But in order to get your divorce here you've got to prove she went off with someone, isn't that right?"

"I could go to Mexico. Divorces are easy there—mental cruelty, incompatibility, lots of vague stuff," said Ernie. "But I can't spare the time."

"It really is hopeless," said Leo. "Funny, I thought Amy was playing around."

"She wasn't," said Ernie, seemingly offended by what Leo had said. "I'm no fool. We weren't suited to each other—I knew that before we got married. But she went on about how she'd kill herself if I wouldn't have her. That sort of thing. We got married and that was a mistake, but no one made a monkey out of me, not even when my marriage was breaking up."

The image suggested a great ship foundering in a boiling sea; but marriage was a flimsy agreement, its only drama was its legality, the image was arrogant. It was the male pride, thought Leo: Ernie denying his cast-off wife's adultery. Her sin was his humiliation. He wanted it all ways.

"Maybe," said Leo, "*she'll* divorce *you*. After all, you were playing around, weren't you?"

"I found a woman I loved," said Ernie. His sincerity reproached Leo.

"It's still adultery," said Leo quickly, trying to cover his embarrassment. "Amy can divorce you for it, can't she?"

"She's up in the clouds," said Ernie. "She's in that *ashram*. You know what they *do* there? They pray, sort of, and meditate, silly things like that. Besides, she's got her money coming every month. They all have in these *ashrams*—they're all rich or divorced there. They don't care; they go around barefoot and write poems. No, she'll never divorce me. I'll have to divorce her, and if I don't do it soon Margo's going to have a bastard in five months' time. A bastard with no passport," Ernie said bitterly.

"But how do you expect to—" Again Ernie did not speak. He waited for Leo to finish. "You can't divorce her. You haven't got any grounds. It's impossible, you said so yourself."

"No, I didn't," said Ernie.

Leo laughed. "Yes, you did!"

"It's possible," said Ernie slowly, "but it's illegal. Did you ever hear of connivance?"

"I suppose conniving is what we're doing now," said Leo.

"Not yet," said Ernie. "Have another drink?" Leo said yes, and Ernie went on. "Amy never committed adultery with anyone and you know it. She wouldn't know where to begin. But if I say she did and can prove it, I can get the divorce—providing she agrees to the whole business."

"You mean, concoct a story about a boy friend she had?"

"They call them corespondents."

"So you have to find a corespondent."

"That's the favor I was going to ask you," said Ernie, and he said it with the same sincerity that had picked at Leo's shame earlier—that reproachful sentence, "I found a woman I loved."

"Me?" said Leo, but couldn't laugh. In a very thin voice he said, "I only met her once."

"Twice," said Ernie. He took out a worn pocket diary and fingered the pages.

Leo remembered the first time. He was new in the country, and, having met Ernie casually in the Rex, Ernie had invited him home for a last drink. Army had made a show of surprise, so wooden and deliberate that the word *theatrical* occurred to Leo; and then she used halting sarcasm: "At least you could have given me a ring and let me know you were bringing someone."

Ernie, much to Leo's discomfort, turned his back on his wife.

Leo said, "I'm terribly sorry if I'm intruding."

"It's not you," Amy had said, "it's him."

It was clear they were not getting on well, and Leo thought: if a man was kind to her she would take him as a lover. Amy left the room. She came back without the ribbon in her hair; her hair was long and alive with the electricity the comb had left in it. She was charming to Leo, got him a drink, lit his cigarette, sat beside him and said, "Have you got pots and pots of money?" when Leo told her he worked at the National and Grindlays.

"No, I'm just a clerk on the foreign exchange side, though I started out on fixed deposits. As a matter of fact,

I'm trying to save enough money so that I can resign in a few years and go back to university."

"I was at Exeter," Amy said. Her reply was pleasing: she was one of the few people who had not said, "At your age?" when he mentioned going back to university. "I did art history, but I read fiction most of the time."

"I read a lot of novels," said Leo. "I'm very fond of—"

"I haven't read a book since—" Here Amy looked at Ernie. "Since I met you."

"Well, children must take up a great deal of your time," said Leo.

"Not here," she said. "We've got slaves—*ayahs*. They do everything, washing, cooking... the children are devoted to them. I've plenty of time. But no ... interest. Are you married?"

Leo shook his head.

"God, how I envy you." Amy closed her eyes and seemed to relax, and Leo took a good look at her. She was pale, small boned, blond as a Swede, with a sharp lean nose and breasts which were probably small—it was hard to tell: she was wearing a loose shirt, one of Ernie's perhaps, and the breasts were only suggestions at the pockets. But she had a lovely fragile face, and with her eyes closed Leo could imagine her head on a pillow.

"You could do a little art history here," Leo said.

"Bongo drums," said Amy contemptuously. "India— that's where the art is. Have you ever been to India, Leo?"

"No." When had he told her his name? "But I've always wanted to go."

"Indians are fabulous creatures—very catlike, I always think, very gentle and smooth," she said, stroking her forearm as she spoke. "Erotic sculpture on temples. Yes! On holy temples! Fantastic things. They worship the *lingam*, you see. You wouldn't believe what they get up to," she said, her eyes flashing. "Look at poor Ernest— he's *blushing!*"

"I am not blushing," said Ernie. "I've heard all this rubbish before. Here, Leo, you want to have a look at those temples? There they are." He pointed to a shelf of large books, boxed editions; art books, Leo knew, even from across the room.

Leo stayed late, talking mostly to Amy. ("My aunt was a character," Amy said at one point, "I once saw her lose her temper and down a whiskey, then smash her glass into the fireplace..."). After twelve Ernie drove Leo back to The Palms. In the car Leo said, "I like your wife. She's very intelligent."

"We're getting a divorce," said Ernie.

It was a statement to which the only tactful response was silence. And Leo knew as Ernie said it that he would have nothing to do with Amy. A married lover, it was said, was a convenient if temporary pleasure; but a woman on the verge of divorce was a terrible risk, a man-eater.

Apparently there *was* a second meeting—Ernie swore it was so, it was marked in his pocket diary—but Leo could not recall it. His interest in Amy died with the news of the divorce. He could remember being a bit sorry, because he had never made love to a married woman, and now his courage failed him. The next time Leo saw Ernie in the Rex, Ernie was with Margo. Leo knew that he could not be friends with both wife and lover. His friendships had to be Ernie's or there would be misunderstandings. And Leo felt mild relief, as if something cloudy and uncertain in his life had disappeared, when Amy went to India. It was a surprising feeling: he barely knew the woman.

"...happens all the time," Ernie was saying. Used to giving orders at the airport and unfamiliar with persuading people to do things, Ernie got excited and distracted telling Leo his idea. He began by saying that he considered it a big favor, but later in the evening he said in a wheedling tone that there was no risk; it was a small thing really, if Leo could see it in its proper perspective. "Look at the paper. Every Thursday they give the court proceedings, and, Christ, they're practically all divorces—even in a little dump like Tanganyika."

Ernie took out his handkerchief and wiped his face. The bar had filled up with seamen who stood, like Ernie, with one foot on the brass rail, glancing around. The regulars were at tables, drinking slowly or not at all, and looking up and commenting when people left or entered through the swinging doors of the bar.

"It's a strange request," Leo said finally. "I don't know what to do."

"There's no one else I can turn to," said Ernie.

"So it really isn't such a small matter, is it?"

"For me, no. It's a life-or-death business for me. But you—God, it's nothing."

"It's a lie, though."

"Oh, yes, I know that," said Ernie. "There's no getting around that."

"And a lie is serious, especially in a legal matter. It's perjury. The whole thing could backfire. I could lose my job at the bank."

"It won't backfire, I swear."

"Everyone knows we're friends. They'll know we made it up."

"That's just it. These divorces, look at them. Who is it that's always named as the third party—it's friends every single time! How else would the wife meet the bloke? The women here don't get out much. The only men they meet are the friends of their husbands. That's how it happens—"

"You mentioned the court proceedings in the paper," said Leo. "I read the paper every day and I've never noticed them, but what bothers me is that other people here probably read them all the time. It would be just like my manager, Farnsworth, to see something like that. If he did I'd be finished."

"Nothing to worry about," said Ernie, becoming eager again. "Don't give that a thought. The editor of the *Standard* is an old pal of mine. I could ask him not to print our names. He'd do it, I know he would. He's a very old friend. I've known him for years."

"Then why don't you name him as corespondent?" said Leo. But he was sorry as soon as he said it.

"Leo, for God's sake!" Ernie said helplessly. "Don't you see I can't? You're my last hope. If you refuse me, I'm stuck—Margo says she'll go away. She'll leave me." Ernie began to sigh softly. "Everyone lets me down, Amy, Margo, my kids—those kids mean a lot to me. You don't have any kids. You don't know what it's like to be away from them. It kills me. Leo, I cry when I think of them—I'm not ashamed, I do." Ernie looked mournfully at Leo and said, "If you did this for for me, you can't imagine what I'd do for you. I'd do anything—" Ernie put his hand on Leo's wrist: the fingers were wet and Leo felt disgust, felt his arm turn clammy as Ernie said, "Just name it—anything—"

"Stop," said Leo, and drew away. "I don't want to make a deal with you," he said. But he said it to convince himself, because at the source of Leo's disgust was the thought that he could have had anything he named; and what was most sinister to him was that he was tempted to ask. But he said: "First put it to Amy. See if she'll agree to it. I take it Margo already agrees. Then—this is crucial—make sure that nothing appears in the *Standard*. Get a definite promise from the editor. If Amy agrees and nothing gets into print, I'll be satisfied."

Ernie beamed. "We're halfway there! Amy's already said yes."

"What? But how did you know I'd agree?"

"I didn't." Ernie grinned. "I just said that I was going to ask you. Here's her letter. I think she means business." Ernie took out a wrinkled aerogram with a pink stamp printed on it. He showed it to Leo, smoothing it on the bar. The handwriting was large, willful, done with a felt marking pen: *I suppose it will happen eventually, so it might as well be your way. Better with Leo than others I could name—he's a nice boy.* There was no signature. Leo folded the aerogram and before he handed it back to Ernie he looked at the unusual return address: *Amy / Ashram / Kolhapur.*

The following Sunday at lunch Ernie was exuberant; he sat a few feet away from the table and held his beer mug on his knee; he laughed loudly and often. He said that he had seen the editor of the *Standard* and got the promise from him; and the lawyer, who was an Indian, knew of the connivance and was drawing up the papers. It was all set.

"Have a beer," said Ernie. "You're not drinking, Leo. Cheer up!"

"I've stopped drinking," said Leo. He hadn't, but the lie was necessary: he wanted nothing from Ernie. On his way to the toilet Leo paid for his own meal. He said he had a headache and went back to The Palms. He did not want Ernie to think that the favor, which already he regretted, could be repaid so easily, or at all. He withdrew into spiteful lassitude and stopped seeing Ernie altogether.

Some weeks after that lunch he was visited by the Indian lawyer, whose name was Chandra and who drove out to The Palms and said softly, "Are you alone?" and then "I've come to deliver a subpoena."

That was ominous; it gave Leo a fright, but Chandra said, "Not to worry—it's just a formality," and stayed for tea. They talked, and as they did, Leo thought: Here is a good man; he would never ask of me what Ernie did. And Leo wished that he had met Chandra instead of Ernie.

Walking to Chandra's car, Leo asked, "Did you know Amy?"

Eagerly Chandra said, "Yes—oh, she was a fine person. She knew a great deal about Indian art—very interested in Indian culture. A graduate, did you know? I was hoping Ernie would try to patch things up—but—"

"He wasn't interested," said Leo.

"I should not say this," said Chandra. "But he did not deserve her."

"You're right," said Leo. And he startled the Indian by saying, "He's a selfish bastard."

Chandra looked warily at Leo and then said good-bye.

He's wondering how I can say that, thought Leo. But the betrayal was not Leo's—it was Ernie's. Ernie's lie had changed Leo and made him restless. He slept badly and had disturbing dreams. In a dream he watched his mother snarling at Ernie and saying, "What have you done to our Leo?" Ernie had replied by sticking his tongue out at the old lady.

A month after he agreed to act as corespondent he admitted his hatred of Ernie to himself. Leo found himself falling into conversations with bank customers who knew Ernie; Leo made a point of calling Ernie a shit, and he encouraged the customers to agree with him. He saw each

of Ernie's enemies—there were quite a number, Leo realized—as his own friends.

Amy as well. He thought of her in ramshackle India
with her two children, living from day to day, in a silent
ashram, in retreat from the world. It seemed a kind of
destitution that he had connived with Ernie in forcing
upon her. How she must hate me, he thought. But Amy
did not know that his part in the conspiracy had ruined
his friendship with Ernie and Margo. Amy didn't know
that in his agreeing to the favor he had accepted the blame
and had had to construct the adultery in his mind in order
to convince himself of his blame. That preoccupation had
begun to obsess and arouse him, almost as if it had
all been true and he was looking back at a recent half-
completed passion which had confused rather than exhausted his feelings.

On an impulse he wrote to her. It was late in the morning, just after coffee, and there were no customers in the
bank because it was raining very hard. He felt lonely, but
writing the letter lifted his spirits. An impediment, the
cramp of language he had sometimes experienced in letter
writing, did not arise this time. The hollowness of letters
with all their inadequate phrases had caused him to stop
writing letters entirely, but the letter to Amy gave him
pleasure. He said, *I rather like the idea of being your
lover.* He said, *I agreed to it because Ernie seemed so
upset, but I don't like him anymore.* He said, in his last
long paragraph, *I'm sitting in the bank and looking out
into the empty foyer and the rainy street*—and that was
especially strange because as he wrote it he did look
around the bank and he tried to explain all the things he
saw to this lonely woman.

She replied. It came quickly and it made Leo realize
that India was just across the water, closer than England.
Amy talked about the children, how brown they had become; about the *ashram*'s activities, the poetry magazine,
the outings, the play school that was being organized. She
said *I've seen those sexy temples, by the way. Fantastic!*
She said she was learning a bit of Hindi. And she finished
her letter with a long paragraph similar to Leo's: *It's late
now and our chickens are silent. The room seems quite*

empty and I'm smoking a cigarette I rolled from the air edition of the Guardian Weekly . . .

That was an aerogram. Her next was many sheets of notepaper in a thick envelope. She unburdened herself and responded to Leo's remark about Ernie (*I don't like him anymore*). She analyzed her marriage more candidly and more fairly than Ernie had ever done; it was a little history, their first meeting and their first disappointments. She said how excited she had been when Leo had come home unexpectedly with Ernie. Leo read, fascinated: she was a victim and here she was alone; Leo had had a part in victimizing her. The deception was like a fishbone in his throat.

Leo wrote Amy a long apology; he asked her to forgive him for agreeing to the lie. He said he was sorry and that if he had it to do over again he would refuse. Amy's reply was: *Don't say that. Don't regret what you've said. You did something fine because you believed Ernie was your friend. I think about you often, Leo, and I sometimes wish we really had gone off together. But it's too late for that now. You're a very sweet person. If you regret what you did, then I'll have to as well. And I don't want that. I'm happy here.*

The bank manager, Farnsworth, frowned at Leo when the coffee boy knocked on the glass partition and said Leo had a telephone call.

"Take your call," said Farnsworth. "I'll check these figures in the meantime."

"Sorry," said Leo. "I'll be right back."

"*Shauri kwisha!*" It was Ernie. "It's all settled! I've just come out of court this minute. It'll be final in three weeks. God, the judge gave me the third degree, asked me how well I knew you and did I know what you were up to . . . Leo, are you there?"

"Yes. Look, I'm busy—"

"I thought you'd laugh when I told you. Say, Leo, is there anything wrong?"

"I'm with the manager. Piles of work—"

"I understand. But what a weight off my shoulders! It's like—just like a big weight lifted off my shoulders. I can breathe again! I feel like celebrating. How about a drink at the Rex?''

"It's not even *noon*, Ernie."

"I can drive right over. Say yes."

"No, I've got work to do."

"Leo, are you feeling all right?"

"I'm fine; I have to go. The manager's waiting. I'll ring you back."

But he didn't ring Ernie back that day; he busied himself with the July figures. And the next day he could have rung, but he had no excuse for neglecting to ring the previous day, none that Ernie would believe. Ernie would still say he was ill or out of sorts. Leo was waiting—for courage, he told himself. He did not want to hear about the divorce and he did not want to see Ernie until he could say what he felt: that Ernie had betrayed him and made him victimize poor Amy.

The third day Ernie rang three times in the morning. Leo told the switchboard operator that if Ernie Grigson rang again—she was to ask for the name—she should tell him that Leo was not available. Leo tried to stay out of sight; he worked in the vault, then in a back office hidden from the street. But late in the afternoon, when he was standing at the front counter and going over his trans-actions on the electric adding machine he sensed someone pause at the window, and he felt it must be Ernie, peering in at him.

It wasn't. Two European ladies had stopped. Leo looked up and they began walking. He didn't recognize them—they were deeply tanned; one wore a headscarf, the other a straw hat—but their gestures were distinct. As they moved along the sidewalk, one looked through the bank's window, directly at him with her broad brown face and bright red lips, and then she quickly looked away and seemed to mumble; the second turned and stared at Leo, shielding her eyes from the glare in a kind of salute. And they walked on. The women did not face each other, but Leo could tell they were speaking. He realized it was Thursday.

Farnsworth came over as Leo was searching the col-umns of the *Standard* for the Court Record. He couldn't find it at first, and when he did find the right column (it resembled the account of a cricket match) it was with difficulty that he located his name among the many there.

"I see we've got our name in the papers, Mockler," said Farnsworth curtly. "Feel like talking about it?"

"No," said Leo.

The Palms was run by a small, neat widow of sixty or more whose husband had been a District Officer in Morogoro. She had a son Leo's age who was an accountant with a public relations firm in Capetown, and usually, before dinner, when Leo was having his drink on the verandah, she joined him and spoke about her son. The other guests tried to avoid her chatter, but Leo was grateful for her company and even listened with patient interest to her reading her son's letters.

But that Thursday, the day Leo's name appeared in the *Standard*'s Court Record, the widow avoided him. She sat at another table with an older resident, a man Leo knew by his nickname, and only once looked at Leo: wickedly, he thought, as if at a traitor. The widow and her elderly companion spoke in rapid whispers, then very loudly and irrelevantly ("Are the Browns in nine?" "I believe they are, yes") to disguise their whispering.

Leo ate alone and felt eyes on him and voices behind him. But he was determined not to be intimidated; after dinner he had his coffee on the verandah instead of the lounge. He turned his back to the people in the bar, which adjoined the verandah, and he faced the sea. The waves lapped, making a breathless splashing, and the palm fronds rattled out of sight, high above him. In the darkness, across that ocean, were India and Amy. He felt like going up to his room and writing her a note. He fought the impulse. If he walked through the bar they would say, "Expect he's going up to write to the other party." They would laugh, because now they believed they knew his closest secret.

A silence consumed the bar sounds; it was as if the sea had mysteriously risen inside and drowned every person there. It happened like that, unnaturally, and the only sounds were the palms and the regular waves and, far-off, one or two barking voices, perhaps of fishermen, the shouts skipping in from the water.

Leo turned to see Ernie walking through the bar. The widow said, "He's outside."

Ernie was at the doorway. He paused and smiled weakly, then came toward Leo with both hands out.

"Leo, I'm sorry," he said, too loud. The people in the bar must have heard because they went silent in a hush once again and Leo could hear the ice rattling in their glasses.

"Go away," the whisper was barely audible. "Don't talk to me here."

"It was the African—"

"Lower your voice," Leo hissed.

"The African," said Ernie. But it was a poor whisper. "At the printery. The stupid bugger forgot what the editor told him about leaving out your name. It's all his fault—"

"Get out," said Leo. He tossed his head. "They're listening."

"I just wanted to tell you that I promised I'd make your bookings—for your long leave. But you never gave me a list of places. You mentioned Vienna, wasn't it? And I forgot the others. So write them down on a piece of paper—"

"All right," said Leo. "Tomorrow. Now do me a favor."

"Yes, of course," said Ernie.

"Get out of here this minute."

"You hate me, don't you? I don't blame you—"

"Ernie!" In his exasperation he raised his voice, and again he heard the ice in the glasses.

"Margo's in the car. She said to thank you," said Ernie.

"Leave by the beach, so they don't see you."

Leo went up to bed by entering the building from the back door, avoiding crossing through the bar. Going up the stairs he thought he heard the widow's voice, "—Indian lawyer came to see him—Knew it then, of course—" her voice was a high, satisfied whine.

Chandra, the widow, the people in the bar, Margo, Amy, Ernie—everyone had got what he wanted out of the divorce, except Leo. All the blame was his and he was suffering for no good reason, as if he alone had been made to sit in a zone of dead air.

* * *

"Coffee?" inquired Farnsworth; Leo said yes, Farnsworth suggested the Gymkhana Club, and Leo knew it was serious: it was in the Billiard Room of the Gymkhana Club that Leo's predecessor, a man who traded currency on the side, was sacked.

Farnsworth was relaxed. He talked about the club, how long he had been a member, all the changes he had seen, how women weren't allowed in the upstairs lounge, how he and others in the old days used to wait every second Friday for the mailboat and the English papers. He leaned forward and said, "Let's take the bull by the horns—"

A man entered the club and, greeting Farnsworth, smiled at Leo.

"You're due for leave in September, am I right?"

"The fifteenth," said Leo.

"Well, I've been thinking," said Farnsworth. "We're not all that busy. I think you can take it a bit earlier than that."

"How soon would that be?" asked Leo.

"Say—within the next fortnight," said Farnsworth. "That'll give you time to make your bookings. If you have any difficulty I'll see what I can do."

"I won't have any trouble with that," said Leo.

"Better settle up with the tax people before you go."

"Aren't I coming back here?" asked Leo.

"Do you *want* to?" Farnsworth looked surprised. "I would have thought not."

"I don't know," said Leo.

"This club has seen its share of scandal," said Farnsworth, and then he smiled. He stood up and put his arm on Leo's shoulder. "I know how it is," he said. "Don't do anything foolish. Things look pretty black to you now. But when you're back in the U.K., everything will seem different. You'll see."

"Can you drop me at the post office? I have a cable to send."

Later in the morning Leo rang Ernie.

"About those plane bookings," Leo said. "I've changed my mind about Beirut—"

"Very sensible," said Ernie. "How do you want me to route you?"

"I'm going to London," said Leo.

"Any stops?"

"Yes," said Leo, "Bombay."

"That's in India," said Ernie. He laughed. "It'll cost a lot extra."

"You can afford it," said Leo.

She had said she would be at the airport, but it was a man who stepped out of the crowd of people with bundles and took Leo by the arm and spoke his name. The man was English; he was dressed like a holy man, in a dusty white robe. His hair was to his shoulders and he had a full beard, the tip of which he clutched as he spoke to Leo: "Amy's told me all about you," he said, but not unkindly. His eyes were extremely gentle, and he held Leo's arm the way one holds an invalid's.

His name was Bob, he said. He was agreeable and helpful, and even recognizing the vast differences in their appearances, Leo felt close to him, saw him as one who had perhaps lived on the periphery of Amy's marriage— probably helped her through the divorce—as Leo had lived alongside Ernie.

"Amy couldn't get away," said Bob. "I'm supposed to take you to the *ashram*." He guided Leo through the crowd and hailed a taxi, and they bumped along through more crowds to a railway station which had the appearance of a busy refugee encampment.

They traveled second class; it was a compromise. Leo wanted first class, which was air-conditioned, and Bob said he always went third. In the train Bob said, "You look petrified!"

"What's that?" asked Leo, glancing out the window.

"A rice field," said Bob.

"No, those naked people."

"Oh, beggars. India's full of them."

They arrived at the *ashram* at night. It was an enormous compound, as plain as an army barracks, surrounded by a freshly painted wall which was floodlit. Amy's house was big, two storied, and she was at the upper window, a white face with darkness behind it.

Leo bounded up the stairs ahead of Bob, but when he saw her his nerve failed and he could not kiss her. Then

Bob was in the room, putting Leo's suitcase against the wall and saying awkwardly, "Well here you are. I'll be going now."

"You're a dear," said Amy. Bob had opened the door. She said, "Narendra?"

"*Baroda*," said Bob, and was away.

"I see you speak the language," said Leo.

"Pardon?" said Amy, and then, "Oh that," and smiled.

She was wearing a sari and gold bangles, and her hair was loosely braided in one thick strand with a tassel at the tip in the Indian style. She was not the person Leo had written to, not the person he had seen at Ernie's house. She was thinner, more angular, awkward, plain even, and her speech was shallow. She was not pretty; she was any English housewife in an Indian costume, and Leo noticed she was smoking and wore a watch.

Leo fumbled with his hands and finally said, "It's a nice house you've got."

"Very old," said Amy. "It belonged to one of the first residents of the *ashram*. A wonderful old man. It's got a fantastic view of the place. You'll see in the morning."

"The kids," said Leo. "Are they asleep?"

"Hours ago," said Amy.

"They didn't wait up," said Leo.

"They didn't know you were coming."

Leo was going to ask why, but didn't. He found it hard to speak to Amy, and it was odd, because he could have written to her very easily; but now he could hardly think of anything to say. She seemed a vague acquaintance, met after a long time, someone he barely knew.

"That's a very handsome oil lamp," said Leo, pointing to the lantern on a carved table; it was the only light in the room.

"Only five rupees at the bazaar," said Amy. "It's solid brass."

"Do you mind if I blow it out?" said Leo. He did not wait for Amy's reply. He walked over, raised the chimney and puffed on it. The room was dark. Leo said, "Where am I going to sleep?"

"Silly," said Amy, and Leo heard the gold bangles clink and saw the sparks from the cigarette being stubbed out.

He heard her walking toward him and saw her arm move outward as if flinging her sari off.

They made love ineptly, in silence, with unsatisfying speed on a rocking *charpoy*. Leo apologized, saying that it had been a long plane journey and that he was tired. And Amy confessed that she was upset, too. It had been dutiful; there was no passion, and Leo felt that he had lived through the act a hundred times already, even to the apology.

He was too excited to sleep, as if he had been rushed through a tunnel, and he told himself that it was the plane. He lay beside Amy and now the room did not seem so dark: he could make out large squares on the ceiling. He still heard the plane, the roar of the landing, and felt the deafening pressure in his ears. He said to himself, "I'm in India," but he felt nothing. All the utterance brought to him was India's flat map shape, the vast red patch, the sharp triangle drooping into green ocean, the black borders and dots of cities. But he would get to know it, and "Yes," he thought, "this could be home for me."

"I want to marry you," said Leo at last.

"No," said Amy, "don't say that."

"Yes," he held her, but felt her struggle slightly.

"I can't," she said; and then pulling away, "What was that?"

Amy rose up on her elbow and looked at the ceiling.

"Did you hear a bicycle?"

"A bicycle?"

"Go look—go to the window," said Amy.

Leo walked to the window. Down in the yard a bicycle leaned on its kickstand. An Indian, hard to make out except for the gleaming whiteness of his *dhoti*, was walking away from it.

"What?" asked Amy.

But Leo did not answer until he had lain down again. "Nothing," he said, "just an Indian."

Amy put her hand to her throat and started to laugh. "It might be Narendra," she said. "My husband." Her laugh was coarse, that stranger's laugh that fitted the new image Leo had of her.

Leo leaped up and looked for his pants, but just as he caught sight of them—they were knotted in a pile ten feet from the bed—he heard feet quickly mounting the stairs.

MEMORIES OF A CURFEW

▲▲▲▲▲▲▲▲▲▲▲▲▲▲▲▲▲▲▲▲▲▲▲▲▲▲▲▲▲▲

IT WAS NOT ODD THAT THE FIRST FEW DAYS OF OUR CUR-
few were enjoyed by most people. It was a welcome
change for us, like the noisy downpour that comes suddenly in January and makes a watery crackle on the street
and ends the dry season. The parties, though these were
now held in the afternoon, had a new topic of conversation. There were many rumors, and repeating these rumors made a kind of tennis match, a serve and return,
each hit slightly more savage than the last. And the landscape of the city outside the fence of our compound was
fascinating to watch. During these first days we stood in
our brightly flowered shirts on our hill; we could see the
palace burning, the soldiers assembling and making people scatter, and we could hear the bursts of gunfire, and
some shouts just outside our fence. We were teachers,
all of us young, and we were in Africa. There were well-
educated ones among us. One of them told me that during
the Roman Empire under the reign of Claudius rich people
and scholars could be carried in litters by *lecticarii*, usually slaves, to camp with servants at a safe distance from
battles; these were curious Romans, men of high station

who, if they so wished, could be present and, between feasts, witness the slaughter.

But the curfew continued, and what were diversions for the first days and weeks became habits. Although people usually showed up for work in the mornings, work in the afternoons almost ceased. There were too many things to be done before the curfew began at nightfall: buses had to be caught, provisions found, and some people had to collect children. We visited the bars so that we could get drunk in the company of other people; we played the slot machines and talked about the curfew, but after two weeks it was a very boring subject.

The people who never went out at night before the curfew was imposed—some Indians with large families used to matinees at the local movie houses, the Africans who did manual labor and some settlers—felt none of the curfew's effects. And there were steady ones who refused to let the curfew get to them; they were impatient with our daily hangovers, our inefficiency, our nervous comments. Our classes were not well-attended. One day I asked casually where our Congolese student was—a dashing figure, he wore a silk scarf and rode a large old motorcycle. I was told that he had been pulled off his motorcycle by a soldier and had been beaten to death with a rifle butt.

We left work early. In the afternoons it was as if everyone was on leave but couldn't afford to go to Nairobi or Mombasa, as if everyone had decided to while away his time at the local bars. At the end of the month no one was paid because the ministry was short-staffed. Some of us ran out of money. The bar owners said they were earning less and less: it was no longer possible for people to drink in bars after dark. They would only have been making the same amount as before, they said, if all the people started drinking in the middle of the morning and kept it up all day. The drinking crowd was a relatively small one, and there were no casual drinkers. Most people in the city stayed at home. They were afraid to stay out after five or so. I tried to get drunk by five-thirty. My memory is of going home drunk, with the dazzling horizontal rays of the sun in my eyes.

The dwindling of time was a strange thing. During the

first weeks of the curfew we took chances; we arrived home just as the soldiers were drifting into the streets. Then we began to give ourselves more time, leaving an hour or more for going home. It might have been because we were drunker and needed more time, but we were also more worried: more people were found dead in the streets each morning when the curfew lifted. For many of us the curfew began in the middle of the afternoon when we hurried to a bar; and it was the drinkers who, soaked into a state of slow motion, took the most chances.

Different prostitutes appeared in the bars. Before the curfew there were ten or fifteen in each bar, most of them young and from the outskirts of Kampala. But the curfew was imposed after two tribes fought; most of the prostitutes had been from these tribes and so went into hiding. Others took their places. Now there were ones from the Coast, there were half-castes, Rwandans, Somalis. I remember the Somalis. There was said to be an Ethiopian at the Crested Crane, but I never saw her; in any case, she would have been very popular. All these women were old and hard, and there were fewer than before. They sat in the bars, futile and left alone, slumped on the broken chairs, waiting, as they had been waiting ever since the curfew started. Whatever other talents a prostitute may have she is still unmatched by any other person in her genius for killing time and staying on the alert for customers. The girls held their glasses in two hands and followed the stumbling drinkers with their eyes. Most of us were not interested in complicating the curfew further by taking one of these girls home. I am sure they never had to wait so long with such dull men.

One afternoon a girl put her hand on mine. Her palm was very rough; she rubbed it on my wrist and when I did not turn away she put it on my leg and asked me if I wanted to go in the back. I said I didn't mind, and so she led me out past the toilets to the back of the bar where there was a little shed. She scuffed across the shed's dirt floor, then stood in a corner and lifted her skirt. Here, she said, come here. I asked her if we had to remain standing up. She said yes. I started to embrace her; she let her head fall back until it touched the wood wall. She still held the hem of her skirt in her hand. Then I said no,

I couldn't nail her against the wall. I saw that the door was still open. She argued for a while and said in Swahili. "Talk, talk, we could have finished by now!" I stepped away, but gave her ten shillings just the same. She spat on it and looked at me fiercely.

Anyone who did not crave a drink went straight home. He took no chances. There were too many rumors of people being beaten up at five or six o'clock by drunken soldiers impatient for the curfew to start. As I say, the drinkers took the risks, and with very little time to spare dashed for their cars and sped home. For many the curfew meant an extra supply of newspapers and magazines; for others it meant an extra case of beer. A neighbor of mine had prostitutes on his hands for days at a time, and once one of the girls' babies in a makeshift cot. Many people talked about rape.

The car accidents were very strange, freak accidents, ones that could only happen during a curfew. One man skidded on a perfectly dry road and drove his car through a billboard six feet wide; dozens of people, as if they had been struck blind, plowed straight across the grass of rotaries. And there were accidents at intersections: not hitting oncoming cars, but smashing into the rears of the cars ahead of them. These rear-end collisions were quite numerous and there were no street sweepers to cope with all the broken glass. It was hard to go a hundred yards without seeing shards, red plastic and white glass, sprinkled on the road. Overturned cars on the verge of the road are rare in Africa, but they became very common around Kampala. Accidents in Africa are usually serious; few end with only a smashed headlight or simple bruises. Either the car is completely ruined or the car and driver disappear. We had some of these fatal accidents during the curfew, but there was also, for the first time, a rash of trivial accidents: broken lights, smashed fenders, bent bumpers, bruised foreheads. I think these were caused by the driver glancing around as he drove, half expecting to see angry people about to stone him, or troops aiming rifles at him. I know I tried to pick out soldiers as I drove along, and I always watched carefully for roadblocks which were so simple (two soldiers and an oil drum) as to be invisible. But it was death to drive through one.

There were so many petty arguments those days. In the bars there were fights over nothing at all; with this, a feeling of tribe rather than color. It was not racism. It was a black revolt, northern Ugandans were killing Bugandans, and neither side was helped to any great extent by anyone who was not black. The lingua franca in Kampala was bad Swahili instead of the usual vernacular which was Luganda. At any other time Swahili would have been a despised language, because only the fringe people used it—refugees, Indians, white men, foreigners. But after the curfew began it was mainly the fringe people who took over the bars.

The curfew reminded many of other curfews they had sat through in their time. During the day, in the bars, if the curfew was mentioned, old-timers piped up contemptuously, "You think *this* is bad? Why, when I was in Leopoldville it was a lot worse than this . . ." Sometimes it was London, Palermo, Alexandria or Tunis, or for the Indians Calcutta, Dacca or Bombay during the Indian emergency. It brought back memories which, though originally violent, had become somewhat glamorous in the long stretch of intervening time: days spent in haggard platoons in the Western Desert, in the dim light of paraffin lamps in Congolese mansions, in London basements with the planes buzzing overhead, in Calcutta with the sound of blood running in the monsoon drains. These men enjoyed talking about the other more effective curfews, and they said that we really didn't know what a curfew was. They had seen men frightened, they said, but this curfew only bored people. Still, I knew then that some time in the future I would recall the curfew—perhaps recall it with the same fanciful distortions that these men added to their own memories. It is so strange. I was in Africa for five years; I remember nothing so clearly as the curfew.

The cripples who sold newspapers at the hotels and down by the Three Stars Bar no longer had to shout and point at their stacks of papers. As soon as the new papers arrived they were sold. The ones from Kenya and Tanzania were in demand since they were printing all the facts and even some of the rumors. The local papers which showed some courage during the first weeks were banned or their reporters beaten up. They now began all their curfew stories, "Things are almost back to normal..."

More and more people began tuning to the External Service of Radio South Africa, and after a time they didn't even apologize. People traded rumors of atrocities (the gorier the story the more knowledgeable the storyteller was considered). No one except the anthropologists chose sides. The political scientists were silent (it was said that as soon as the tribal dispute started a half a dozen doctoral dissertations were rendered invalid). We waited for the curfew to end. But the weeks passed and the curfew stayed the same. At night there was stillness where there had been the rush of traffic in town, the odd shout, or the babbling of idle boys in the streets. Barking dogs and the honk and cackle of herons in our trees replaced the human noises. The jungle had started to move in. Every hour on the hour the air was thunderous with the sound of news broadcasts, but after that, at our compound, you could stand on the hill and hear nothing. Lights flashed soundlessly and to no purpose. Nothing outside the fence moved. Viewed from the hill the curfew seemed a success.

"This is your friend?" asked the Somali girl in Swahili.

The Watusi next to her ignored the question. He turned to me, "*C'est ma fille, Habiba.*" When I looked at the girl he said in Swahili, "Yes, my friend Paul—*rafiki wangu.*"

"*Très jolie,*" I said, and in English, "Where'd you find her?"

"*Sur la rue!*" He laughed.

For the rest of the evening we spoke in three languages, and when Habiba's friend, Fatma the Arab, joined us the girls spoke their own mixture of Swahili and Arabic. Gestures also became necessary.

I did not know the Watusi boy well. We had spoken together, our French was equally bad, but it was interlarded with enough Swahili and English for us to understand each other. And that was a strange enough *patois* to create a bewildered silence around us in the bar. I knew he was from Burundi; he claimed a vague royal connection—that was one of the first things he had told me. I had bought him a drink. His name was Jean. His surname had seven syllables.

He leaned over. "She has a sister," he said.

At six o'clock we drove to the Somali section of town, a slum like all the sections inhabited by refugees. Even the moneyed refugees—the fugitive *bhang* peddlers, the smugglers—seemed to prefer the anonymity of slums. Habiba's sister came out. She was tall, wearing a veil and silk trousers, but with that sable grace—long necked, eyes darting over the veil, thin, finely made hands, a jewel in her nostril—that makes Somali women the most desired in Africa. Jean talked to her in Swahili. I smoked and looked around.

There were about a dozen Somali families in this compound of cement sheds; they leaned against the walls, talked in groups, sat in the deep mud ruts that coursed through the yard, eroded in the last rain. Some men at the windows of the sheds sent little boys over to beg from us. We refused to give them any money, but one begged a cigarette from me which he quickly passed to a tough-looking man who squatted in a doorway.

Habiba came back to the car and said it was impossible for her sister to come with us. The men would be angry. The Somali men, forced by the curfew to meander about the yard of their compound, the ones sending little boys to beg from us and chewing the stems of a green narcotic weed (the style was the hillbilly's, but the result was delirium)—these refugees with nothing to do and nowhere to go might lose their tempers and kill us if they saw two of their girls leaving with strangers. They could easily block the drive that led out of the compound; they would have had no trouble stopping our car and beating us. They had nothing to lose. Besides, they were within their rights to stop us. Habiba had a husband, now on a trip (she said) upcountry; technically these other Somali men were her guardians until her husband returned. Two dead men found in a drain. It would not have been a very strange sight. Corpses turned up regularly as the curfew was lifted each morning.

Habiba got into the car and we drove away. I expected a brick to be tossed through the back window, but nothing happened. Several men glared at us; some little boys shouted what could only have been obscenities.

Take a left, take a right, down this street, left again, chattered Habiba in Swahili. I drove slowly; she pointed to a ramshackle cement house with a wooden verandah pocked by woodworm and almost entirely rotted at the base. Some half-caste children were playing nearby, chasing each other. The racial mixtures were apparent: Arab-African, Indian-Somali, white-Arab. The texture of the hair told, the blotched skin; the half-African children had heavy, colorless lips. We entered the house and sat in a cluttered front room. There were pictures on the walls, film stars, a calendar in Arabic, and other calendar pictures of huntsmen in riding gear and stiff squarish dogs. And there was a picture of the ruler whose palace had been attacked. No one knew whether he had been shot or managed to escape.

Some half-castes and Arabs drifted in and out of a back room to look at us, the visitors, and finally Fatma came. She was unlike Habiba, not ugly, but small, tired-looking and—the word occurred to me as I looked at her in that cluttered front room—dry. Habiba was very black, with a sharp nose, large, soft eyes and long, shapely legs; Fatma was small, ageless in a shriveled way, with frizzed hair and one foreshortened leg which made her limp slightly. Her eyes were weary with lines; she could have been young and yet she seemed to have no age. She was cautious—now seated and carefully smoothing her silk wrappings, not out of coyness but out of the damaged reflex of pride that comes with generations of poverty. Even the small children in that room looked as concerned as little old men. I felt like a refugee myself who, moving from slum to slum, took care in an aimless, pointless way. Fatma offered us tea.

At that moment I changed my seat. I moved into a chair with my back to the wall. I know why I did it: I was sitting in front of a window and I had the feeling that I was going to be shot in the back of the head by a stray bullet. During the curfew there was always gunfire in Kampala. That was four years ago, and in Africa, but I am still uneasy sitting near windows.

"No time for tea," Jean said in Swahili. He pointed to his watch and said, "Curfew starts right now."

Fatma left the room and Jean nudged me. "That girl," he said in English, "I support her."

"Comment?"

"La fille est supportable, non?"

We had only fifteen minutes to get back. We drove immediately to a shop and bought some food and a case of beer, then hurried back to my apartment and locked ourselves in. It was precisely seven when we started drinking. The girls, although Moslems, also drank. They said they could drink alcohol "except during prayers."

As time passed the conversation lapsed and there was only an occasional gulp to break the silence. We had run through their life stories very quickly. Habiba was eighteen, born in Somalia. She came to Uganda because of the border war with Kenya which prevented her from living in her own district or migrating to Kenya where she was an enemy. She married in Kampala. Her husband was away most of the time; in the Congo, she thought, but she was not sure. Fatma's parents were dead, she was twenty-two, not married. She was from Mombasa but liked Kampala because, as she said, it was green. The rest of the conversation was a whispered mixture of Arabic and Swahili which the girls spoke, and the French-English-Swahili which Jean and I spoke. Once we turned on the radio and got Radio Rwanda. Jean insisted on switching it off because the commentator was speaking the language of the Bahutu, who were formerly the slaves of Jean's tribe. That tribal war, that massacre, that curfew had been in 1963.

Jean told me what ugly swine the Bahutu were and how he could not stand any Bantu tribe. He squashed his nose with his palm and imitated what I presumed to be a Hutu speaking. He said, "But these girls—very *Hamite*." He traced the profile of a sharp nose on his face.

The girls asked him what he was talking about. He explained, and they both laughed and offered some stories. They talked about the Africans who lived near them; Fatma described the fatal beating of a man who had broken the curfew. Habiba had seen an African man stripped naked and made to run home. She mimicked the man's worried face and flailed her long arms. "Curfew, curfew," she said.

Jean suddenly stood and took Habiba by the arm. He led her to a back room. It was eight o'clock. I asked Fatma if she was ready. She said yes. She could have been a trained bird, brittle and obedient. She limped beside me into the bedroom.

At eleven I wandered into the living room for another drink. Jean was there with his feet up. He asked me how things were going. We drank for a while, then I asked him if he was interested in going for a walk. If we went to sleep now, I said, we'd have to get up at four or five. We switched off all the lights, made sure the girls were asleep, and went out.

The silence outside was absolute. Our shoes clacking on the stones in the road made the only sound and, at intervals, the city opened up to us through gaps in the bushes along the road. Lights can appear to beckon, to call in almost a human fashion, like the strings of flashing lights at deserted country fairs in the United States. The lights cried out. But we were safe inside the large compound; no one could touch us.

When we were coming back to my apartment an idea occurred to me. I pointed to the dark windows and said, choosing my words carefully, "Supposing we just went in there without turning on any lights . . . Do you think the girls would notice if we changed rooms?"

"*Changez de chambres?*"

"*Je veux dire, changez de filles.*"

He laughed, a drunken sort of sputtering, then explained the plan back to me, adding, "*Est-ce que c'est cela que vous voulez faire?*"

"*Cela me serait egal, et vous?*"

Habiba was amused when she discovered, awaking as the act of love began, that someone else was on top of her. She laughed deep in her throat; this seemed to relax her, and she hugged me and sighed.

Jean was waiting in the hallway when I walked out an hour later. He was helpless with suppressed giggling. We stood there in the darkness, our clothes slung over our shoulders, not speaking but communicating somehow in a wordless giddiness which might have been shame. At the time I thought it was a monstrous game, like a child's, but hardly even erotic, played to kill time and defeat fear and loneliness—something the curfew demanded.

But after the curfew ended, I changed my mind. I had not been playing; all my gestures had been scared and serious. I stopped trusting. I became rather jumpy and found I could not teach anymore. And so I left Africa, deciding I needed a rest, and checked into a hotel in the south of France. One day while I was sunning myself at the swimming pool, a large black man appeared between two flowering bushes at the far end. He was wearing a light suit and he carried a briefcase. He walked heavily along the poolside, toward me, and I imagined for a moment—a moment in which the memory of the curfew rubbed and mumbled—that he had come to kill me. He passed by me and entered the bar. He was, I found out later, a famous Nigerian economist. He stayed at the hotel for three days, and committed no outrage.

BIOGRAPHICAL NOTES
FOR FOUR AMERICAN POETS

^^^^^^^^^^^^^^^^^^^^^^^^^^^^^

"ROBERT FROST WAS SITTING RIGHT WHERE I AM NOW,"
said Denton Fuller, the American poet, in Amherst. "In
this very rocking chair—"

In *The Hub*, A Magazine of Verse, Fuller's biographical
note read: *Born Conway, N.H., 1922; attended Green
Mountain School and Bowdoin College; after graduation,
"army and Byronesque ramblings." Worked for PORT-
LAND (Me.) HERALD, wrote verse late at night and far
into the morning on rolls of newsprint. First book* No
News *(1946) followed by* Barefoot Boy *(1949);* Good
Fences *(1956) won Mr. Fuller a John Wheeler Fellowship.
He is presently teaching part-time and writing. Married,
two daughters. Hobbies: mushrooms, dogs, farming.*

"—just staring off this porch, looking meaningfully at
the Common there. He could have been Tiresias, with his
shock of white hair and that wise old clapboard face. And
he said to me, 'Denton, I once ran away from this college—there were so many things I wanted to do.'"

"And miles to go before he slept," murmured Wilbur
Parsons, the American poet.

In *The Hub*, Parsons's biographical note read: *Born
Worcester, Mass., 1918; educated Worcester Academy*

and Harvard Business School; Rhodes Scholar (Oxford University, England) 1940–41; published first book shortly after joining Homemakers Mutual Insurance Co. (Boston and New York, with branches around the world); now Executive Vice-President of this company. In 1949 Mr. Parsons founded The Hub, *A Magazine of Verse, which he edits today when the world of finance is too much with him. Author of* The Muse and Mammon *(1943),* Predilections *(1950) and* Bull and Bear *(1957).* Curtain Raisers *(1965) is a collection of Mr. Parsons's translations from the Russian of Iosip Brodsky. Married, no children. Hobbies: wines, travel, yachting, golf.*

"I can't say that I knew Frost," Parsons went on. "Of course we chatted dozens of times at Breadloaf. And I was responsible for putting lots of his stuff in *The Hub*. He was a marvelous old man. My wife used to say he was salty."

"Oh, he was an old salt," said Denton Fuller. "He could have been the skipper of some great sailing ship."

"I always thought of him as the yeast at Breadloaf," said Sumner Bean, the American poet. "I mean no disrespect."

In *The Hub*, Bean's biographical note read: *Born Kennebunkport, Me., 1921; educated at The Friends School, Cambridge, and Antioch College. A conscientious objector, Mr. Bean served as an ambulance driver, 1942–45; published his war poems,* Back to Front *(1946), and taught for two years in Kyoto, Japan, 1949–51; published* Enemies No More *(1953). For some years he has been working on a verse play set at the time of Hiroshima and tentatively titled* Seeing the Light. *Presently teaching at Webster Friends College (Webster, Mass.). Married, four sons and a daughter. Hobbies: cycling, swimming, baking bread. Describes himself as "The oldest 'younger poet' in the U.S.A."*

"It was his sense of humor," said Wilbur Parsons.

"He said he wrote his poems in couplets"—Sumner Bean grinned brightly—"because that's how the world goes on—by coupling!"

"I remember him chaffing Ciardi for telling him what 'The Road Not Taken' meant," said Fuller. "I mean, symbolically, you see. He would say—"

Here Stanley Gold, the American poet, said, "For God's sake, how long is this going on! You talk about Frost as if he was some old local druggist that made great banana splits."

Gold's biographical note was long and breezy, and usually magazines only printed part of it. *The Hub* had never done that much, for Gold had never published there. But the *New Republic, Harper's, Commentary* and (once) *The New Yorker* had published his poems. His fullest biographical note appeared in the *Beloit Poetry Journal: Born N.Y.C., 1931. Educated P.S. 119 (Flatbush) and Brooklyn College. Awarded M.A. Columbia, 1955. Worked as bus boy, steam-fitter, garage mechanic, welfare inspector, high school teacher. Nervous breakdown (1958)* [once, a magazine in Iowa printed this as if it was the title of a book of poems] *followed by a period of intensive "lenitive, purgative, cathartic" writing. Mr. Gold is the author of* The Jew's Ruse *(1960),* Hitler Riddles *(1962). A Guggenheim Fellow in 1965, Mr. Gold traveled to Israel, which resulted in* Ruthless in Gaza *(1967), a travel diary. Divorced, no hobbies.*

"What do you mean by that?" demanded Fuller.

"That's how the world goes on, by coupling. Doesn't that sound a little *cute* to you? There was a lot of schmaltz in Frost. You must be kidding about Tiresias. Let's face it, Frost was a Yankee Harry Golden. You know, *Enjoy, Enjoy!* Except that Frost was writing for English department phonies, not fat Jews at Grossingers', so he wrote *Provide, Provide!* But it's the same cruddy ethos." Stanley Gold started to recite "Birches" in a Yiddish accent ("Ven I zee boiches...") but was cut off sharply by Fuller.

"You never met Frost, did you?" snapped Fuller.

"Me?" Stanley Gold shrugged under the severe gazes of the others. "I don't know what you mean by met. I heard him recite his poems at the Y.M.H.A. in Manhattan. Then I saw him on television, at Kennedy's inauguration. His papers blew off the podium, remember? I saw him at Trilling's house, too, I forget when. He read his poems in a crackly voice, a kind of Spencer Tracy croak—"

Wilbur Parsons's finger had been pointed directly at

Gold's chin for some minutes. Gold frowned at the finger and cocked his head to the side comically. But no one laughed.

"I'll tell you something," said Parsons. "You don't know the first thing about Frost and I'll tell you how I know and you can correct me if I'm wrong, Denton." Parsons paused, sipped his drink, then said simply, "Frost never recited his poems to anyone, anywhere."

"I heard him," said Gold. "At the Y.M.H.A. Then at Trilling's. I *heard* him recite his poems, I'm telling you. 'Boiches,' for example."

"Frost never recited his poems," Parsons continued, as if Gold had not said anything. "Frost used to . . . *say* . . . his poems. Am I right, Denton?"

"Absolutely, Wilbur. That's what he called it." Denton Fuller jutted his jaw out and said in a rasping voice, "I am now going to say a poem called 'Desert Places.'"

"He never *recited*, he always *said* his poems," Parsons recited.

"Said, read," Gold muttered. "It's pretty cute, pretty stagy."

"Would you put your *Hitler Riddles* next to *A Boy's Will*?" Parsons challenged.

"What is this, some kind of stock market?" Gold snarled. Then he fell silent.

Sumner Bean steered the conversation to Robert Lowell's world view. He ordered drinks for everyone, a grapefruit juice for himself.

The day had not started badly. In the car, driving to Bradley Field to meet Parsons's plane, Fuller had said to Bean, "I've been excited about this seminar for weeks. I was writing night and day, night and day. I was on to something very big and very important to me personally. I knew I had to finish it in time for the seminar, so I could show you. And by God I *did* finish it. It's back at the hotel. Frankly speaking I think it's the best thing I've done, but I'll let you be the judge of that."

"I want to see it, Denton. You know I do." Sumner Bean's gentle Quaker voice soothed Fuller.

"You look at this poem," said Fuller. "But be brutal, tear it to pieces if you want to."

Sumner Bean smiled.

Fuller relaxed and drove the car with confidence, reducing his speed on the thinly iced road. "Working like a mule," he said. "I shut myself off completely when I work. Don't talk to a soul. Just pick at my food. I go for long walks. Refuse to answer the telephone."

"We don't have a telephone," said Sumner Bean. As he said it he sensed a stiffening in Fuller and was jogged by a thumped throttle. He realized he had hurt Fuller in making the nonownership of a telephone somehow virtuous. "We're planning to get one installed, though," he lied. "Say, Denton, how's the farm?"

"Big Bertha's calved," said Fuller proudly, recovering.

"What a lovely verb," said Bean. *"Calved."*

"Well, it's mine," said Fuller, and he lifted his head and recited, "'All around the green farm the acres are waking, / And hard by her stanchion old Bertha's calved—'"

"I thought that sounded familiar," said Bean.

"'Good Fences,'" said Fuller, and he cheered up.

Parsons arrived tanned, an odd figure crossing the snow-swept runway, with jaunty, befeathered alpine hat and a trim topcoat, overnight bag and briefcase. He shook hands: "Denton, Sumner, good to see you again," and said that he had just returned from Nassau, where he had "dickered with some offshore properties, did a little fishing, and worked on a poem."

"You're brown as a berry," said Fuller.

"But not as dark as Berryman," said Bean.

"Ha-ha," said Parsons. "But odd you should mention him. I was talking with John just this morning in New York. I'm anthologizing him."

"How's business?" asked Fuller when they were in the car and driving toward Amherst.

Parsons, in the back seat, said, "I'm working on a sonnet."

"I meant your company."

"Oh, *that*," laughed Parsons. "Going great guns. I'm negotiating a bauxite contract."

"How do you do it," said Bean with admiration. "It's all I can do to keep up with marking the freshman themes. And you, with your bauxite and ballads!"

"There's a title for you, Wilbur," said Fuller.

But Parsons had leaned forward, resting his forearms on the top of the front seat, near Sumner Bean. He was looking meditatively at the dashboard. "How do I do it? Let me ask you something: how did Wallace Stevens do it?"

"I've always wondered," said Sumner Bean.

"I'll tell you," said Parsons. "My secretary, Martha, takes my first draft down in shorthand, and then types it up with wide margins, triple spaced. I work like blazes on that, penciling in words, crossing things out, adding new stuff. It's a beautiful mess when I'm through with it, like one of Balzac's galley proofs."

"The Buffalo Library's buying work sheets," said Fuller. "They're paying well for them, too."

"They've got some of mine," said Parsons, "some early drafts of *The Muse and Mammon*. They've got some graduate students doing their Ph.D.'s on my work. But as I was saying, Martha's the only one who can read my handwriting. I give her my fussed-up page and she hands me back a clean copy. I mess that one up; she does another. And that's the way it goes. I keep working the thing into shape until it's letter-perfect. And, you know, the poem I start with is never the poem I finish up with— it's a completely different poem. Take that sonnet I started in Nassau. That will keep changing and changing. I'll give it to Martha on Monday. She says I'm a perfectionist. I don't know what I'd do if she ever left the firm."

"How did Wallace Stevens do it?" asked Sumner Bean.

"Well, that's my point. Exactly the same way," said Parsons. "But he did it in Key West."

"Eliot had his typist, too," said Bean. He chuckled.

Parsons dozed, his jaunty hat over his eyes, his hands folded across his briefcase.

"I carry all sorts of scraps of paper around with me," said Fuller eagerly. "Some I carry around for years, with little bits and pieces of writing on them, phrases, words, you see. They don't mean a thing to anyone else: it's a kind of code. Then, when I get a free month, I go up to the farm and sit down and put it all together, scratching away like mad on yellow legal-size paper with a four-B pencil."

"I use a typewriter, an old Remington," said Bean.

"It's so mysterious, writing poems," said Fuller. "I don't know how it happens. It's a kind of magic, I guess."

"I haven't written a poem in three years," said Bean sadly. "Really, I haven't. It's terrible, isn't it?"

Fuller could not think of any words of consolation for Bean at first. But diving across a dry stretch of road near the greenhouses on the Amherst outskirts, Fuller was inspired. He spoke to the snowy corrugations of a distant field: "We all have our dry patches. Be patient. It'll come bubbling up when the mood takes you."

After lunch (roast chicken, new potatoes, fresh corn, Indian pudding) they adjourned to the hotel piazza, where in the chill afternoon air they sat and waited for Stanley Gold, who had said he would be driving up from New York in his own car.

"They must think we're a bunch of crazy bohemian poets," said Parsons, rubbing his hands and tossing his head in the direction of nearby windows. Lunching couples sat at festive tables, watched the poets, and chewed. "They're staring at us because we're doing what we damn please."

"I was looking at that tree," said Fuller reflectively. "It's a willow tree. When I was a boy I used to pretend I was a bell ringer and pull the branches of willow trees down, *dong-dong-dong*."

"A weeping willow," said Bean.

"It's supposed to be a sad tree," said Parsons. "But I don't think of it as a sad tree. For me it's a happy tree, Look at it."

Rooted in the Common, the tree was a cold fountain of black leafless wires, the trunk battered and icy.

"Yes, it is a happy tree," said Fuller. "Not a weeping tree at all."

"It droops, of course," said Parsons. "But that's part of its charm. No, it's not a sad tree."

"Like"—Bean struggled with a phrase—"like . . . so many . . . graceful . . ." He could not go on. He had not written a poem for three years. He drank his juice.

When Stanley Gold arrived they were still watching the tree and discussing the happy aspect it presented. Gold seated himself with them (he wore a thick woolen scarf and an army jacket; his hair was wild and bushy, his ears bright red, his glasses iced with frozen crystal needles of scattered breath). He listened for a while, blowing on his fingers, then asked, "Say, in the winter, how can you tell which trees are dead and which aren't?" and here the conversation turned to Robert Frost.

At six-fifteen that same evening on the steps of the Amherst town hall, Parsons, Fuller and Bean waited for Stanley Gold. They had arranged to meet at six; Fuller said that he had "a little surprise" for them before their early meal, a pizza and a pitcher of beer at one of the local hangouts. Parsons said he had not had a pizza for years; Bean said he was game; Gold had nodded and said (rather too quickly, Fuller thought), "Okay, okay." Parsons said that it was customary for the English Department sponsoring such seminars to give a cocktail party before the talks and a little cold buffet afterward ("They had quite a spread for me when I read at Swarthmore"), but added that he was frankly quite anxious to see what Fuller's surprise was. There would be drinks at Professor Bloodworth's after the evening session. At six-twenty Fuller said he didn't think Gold would show.

"Nothing gold can stay," said Bean. He was dressed for the weather: a fur hat and thick duffel coat, corduroy trousers stuck in high, freshly oiled lumberjack boots, heavy woolen mittens. The others paid no attention to Bean's compulsive pun. Bean himself had been ten minutes late: Parsons, watching Bean approach, had said, "Look, Denton, he even *dresses* like a Quaker!" Fuller had replied, "Sumner's got a heart of gold," and Parsons quipped, "Let's hope not." They were laughing softly even as Bean joined them.

Now Parsons was saying, "I'd never take that young man on my firm. Oh, I know he's supposed to be a good poet—very popular with campus audiences, they say—but in business punctuality is essential. If he were coming for an interview right now I would simply say to him, 'Sorry, the post has been filled by a prompt applicant,' and that, my friends, would be that. I say we push off."

"Let's give him another five minutes," said Fuller,

flashing his watch crystal toward the streetlamp and trying to read it. "Starting now."

"What's the hurry?" Bean asked inoffensively. "Maybe he's doing something important, a call from home or something."

"Very charitable of you, Sumner," said Parsons, "but don't waste your charity. Five'll get you ten he's inside the hotel sitting on his butt. I'm telling you, I know an unreliable man when I see one. Besides, he's divorced—so we know he's not calling his wife, don't we?"

Bean did not reply.

"Dylan Thomas was always late," said Fuller. He detected that Bean disapproved of Parsons's remark about Gold's divorce. Bean made a point of counseling unhappy couples and, discouraging gossip, trying to patch things up.

"Stanley Gold is not Dylan Thomas," said Parsons. "I met Dylan at Williams College back in—was it fifty-two? You could excuse that man for anything, anything at all." Parsons blew a jet of steamy breath into the night air and said, "I've had it. Gentlemen, shall we lead on?"

"I don't see," said Bean, "how you can be so hard on Stanley. He strikes me as a very sincere person. And I've read his poems. They're darned good."

"Well, I haven't read as many of his poems as you have, I'm sure. He's never sent any to *The Hub*," said Parsons, aggrieved. "But I'll tell you something. I stand here waiting for him and I say to myself: This isn't how poems get written. With poetry it's fish or cut bait. It takes discipline, application, plain old work. Gold would probably call me an old fogy for saying this: it takes a lot of things that young man doesn't have."

"I don't think Stanley would call you an old fogy," said Bean.

Parsons continued. "That's why Stevens will always be a greater poet for me than, say, Hart Crane. One basic reason is that Stevens knew about discipline, and there was no nonsense about it. He ordered his life. He invested wisely. He ordered his poems. There's something very, very American about that. Hart Crane was a sot. Granted, his death was tragic. I'm not saying it wasn't. But Wallace

Stevens knew how a poem is made, the way real poets do.''

"I haven't written a poem for three years," said Bean. He said it with a certain pride.

"Marilyn Monroe was always late," said Fuller. "I'm thinking of writing a poem about her. She was America.''

"She had a lot of talent," said Parsons. "But hasn't someone already done a poem about her? Was it Thom Gunn?''

"He did Elvis Presley," said Fuller, piqued.

"They say Marilyn Monroe had a very unhappy childhood," said Bean.

"The worst," said Fuller. "Boy, could I tell you some stories. They'd stand your hair on end.''

Bean had been watching the distant sidewalk. He saw a figure loping along. He said, "I think that's Gold, isn't it? He's headed in this direction.''

Parsons squinted. "Could be." He turned to Bean. "I tell you what. I'm going to ask him where he's been. Watch him squirm. A fellow like that never gets asked why he's late. It'll be a good experience for him.''

"You might call this a threat," said Bean in a steady voice, facing the much taller Parsons, "but if you ask him that I will go straight back to the hotel in protest. You have no right to ask that man for an explanation. None whatsoever.''

Parsons turned away. When Gold came near and Fuller led the way down the icy sidewalk, Parsons paired up with Fuller and Gold fell in with Bean. The four poets shuffled, so as not to fall.

"You see a lot of stars around here," said Gold.

Bean obligingly indicated several constellations.

Up front Parsons talked about Nassau. They walked two hundred yards, then Fuller said to stop right where they were and to look across the street. There was a high wall of shrubbery—evergreens—some bare trees, and just visible the large-windowed top floor of a very old house. Gold and Bean caught up. They all stared at the house.

"What I want you to look at," said Fuller, "is that upper right-hand window over there." He pointed to the window with a gloved hand. The window gleamed black.

"A great poet lived there her whole life. Barely stirred from her room. Great poems were written right up there behind that window." Fuller paused, saying with some emotion, "The poems of Emily Dickinson."

"When I was reading my poems in England," said Parsons, "an Englishman came up to me and said, 'I know you have Edna Ferber, but we have Emily Brontë.' I looked him straight in the eye and said, 'We have Emily Dickinson, and they don't come any better than that.' He shut up, of course."

But Bean had started reciting "Much Madness is divinest Sense" and Parsons's story went unnoticed. Fuller followed with "After great pain, a formal feeling comes," and Parsons, with a glance at Gold, recited "A narrow fellow in the grass." And then they went for their pizza.

The seminar ("Poetry: Meaning and Being") was held in the overheated chapel. The poets spoke in turn. With a rustic twinkle in his eye, Fuller talked about his own poems ("Who knows where a poem comes from?") and his ardent cultivation of cabbages ("And that's a kind of creating, too!"). Parsons was candid about the rat race and said there was no money in poetry, but writing poems was "a lot cheaper than paying five grand to a headshrinker"; he told about his secretary and how he often composed poems right in Wall Street itself ("Who needs a vernal wood?"); and he read some of his Russian translations. Bean spoke movingly of Vietnam: "At this moment a young poet in Bienhoa is trying to unstick fiery napalm from his fingers," and he finished with a sequence of verses written not by himself (he confessed his three-year barrenness) but by Ho Chi Minh, Dag Hammarskjöld, Mao Tse-tung, the wife of Harold Wilson, Léopold Senghor and John Kennedy. The Kennedy was prose, but he read it as verse. Gold shouted love lyrics scattered with references to elimination; he refused to comment on or explain any of them. At the end of the seminar the questions, mumbled by admiring students, hairy and in greasy jackets, were all directed at Gold. The chairman, closing the seminar, said confidently, "I think we've all learned something this evening," and he led the four poets to a party at Professor Bloodworth's.

The party continued for nearly three hours, climaxing in a magical but unfortunate sudden hush in the din during which the young wife of a graduate student was heard in an insistent voice to say, "I wouldn't mind if Mailer buggered me!" Guests winced. One associate professor said, "Well, I guess that about wraps it up." There was laughter; the room emptied.

At the front door, Mrs. Dorothy Margoulies, M.A. candidate ("Ferlinghetti and the Coney Island Ethos") and wife of the witty associate professor, said good night to Parsons and Fuller. She was moved to a violent nervous shuddering. She caught her breath and said, "I haven't felt this way since William Golding read here. I don't know what to say—"

She prattled. In the living room someone clinked ashtrays, emptying them; in the kitchen, someone else was stacking dishes in the plastic-basket innards of an automatic dishwasher; in the study, Sumner Bean thumbed a book he had been wait-listed for at the Webster Library for months; Stanley Gold, slumped in a wing chair, tried to tune in on the conversation at the door.

"—*So* enjoyed your talks and readings, and I can't *tell* you how much—" There was a false pause as her voice fell, the low pitch making a purring silence. Gold heard his name, and laughter.

Then Parsons. "—Must get back to New York tomorrow—" A pause. "—No, ha-ha, not exactly. You see, Stevens worked in Connecticut. I guess that's your only major difference."

"My farm's at Ripton," said Fuller. "I'm going to shoot right up there as fast as I can."

In a cheerful frame of mind, Parsons and Fuller entered the living room. Stanley Gold stared at Parsons, then asked, "*Kak viy pozhivaete*?"

"I beg your pardon," said Parsons, still wearing the warm grin with which he had sent off the grateful Mrs. Margoulies.

"It's Russian," said Gold.

"If you say so," said Parsons. He looked at his watch.

"It's a question."

"I thought I detected an interrogatory note there somewhere," said Parsons. He checked his watch again.

"So what's your reply?"

"My reply"—and here Parsons glanced at Professor Bloodworth and Fuller—"is I don't know what the hell you're up to, but I'm going back to the hotel and get some sleep or I won't be able to do a lick of work tomorrow."

"Why?" Gold's eyes were big behind thick lenses. "Are you thinking of doing a few translations tomorrow?"

"See here," Parsons began.

But Gold had already started speaking: "I'd like to know where the hell you get the right to pretend you do translations from a language you don't know! Just tell me that and I'll be satisfied."

"Auden translated *Markings* and he doesn't know a word of Swedish. He said so." Bean called from the study.

"Shakespeare didn't speak Latin or Greek," said Fuller. "And he—"

"A little Latin and less Greek," said Bloodworth in humorous reproof. He gave the quotation its source.

"Settle down, young fellow," said Parsons. "Oh, I know you're thinking I'm a faker. But, hell, Kunitz doesn't speak Russian."

"I'm not talking about Kunitz. I'm talking about you, Daddy Warbucks."

"If you can't talk in a civil manner I'm not going on with this. You have no right to ask me for an explanation for anything. I stand by my poems and my magazine. If you think you can do a better translation of Brodsky you're welcome to try." Parsons calmed himself and added, "And while you're at it, you can send your poems to *The Hub*. We'd be mighty pleased to get them. You've never sent us any, you know."

"And I don't intend to," said Gold.

"Come on, son," said Fuller, as if to a juvenile delinquent. "Parsons is trying to help you."

"Your magazine is financed by you, isn't it?" said Gold to Parsons; he did not wait for a reply. "And your money comes from your insurance company, right? A company that for the past five years has owned controlling interest in a chemical plant that produces defoliant for the Defense Department! Who are you trying to kid!"

"Hold on a minute," said Parsons.

Bean appeared at the study door. "Say, Wilbur, that's a very serious charge. You never told me anything about that."

"Let me say this," said Parsons. "We're Americans. Each of us, in his own way, directly or indirectly, whether we want to or not, has something to do with war. I'll give you a small example. Do you know where your tax money goes?"

"I don't pay taxes," said Gold. "I don't earn enough."

"I haven't paid taxes for ten years," said Bean. "It's down-right immoral, contributing to a corrupt government. I'm prepared to go to jail if necessary."

"You're off your head," said Parsons to Bean. "It's your business, I know that. But if you ask me—"

"It's been a long day," said Fuller sheepishly to Bloodworth.

"—I've endowed a lot of magazines," Parsons was saying, "a hell of a lot of them. That doesn't mean I agree with their editorial policies, no indeed! I have nothing but respect for Dr. Spock's views, don't think I haven't—"

"What about your chemical plant?" asked Bean.

"I didn't come here to talk shop," said Parsons. "I came here as a poet. We're all poets. I don't know why we're behaving like this if we're poets." He stopped momentarily and looked at Bean's face, Gold's face, Fuller's face; he saw something witless and fatigued on each one. He guessed that the same thing showed on his own face. He spoke again, his tongue feeling very large in his mouth. "Come to my office. I can explain everything." He turned to Gold. "And as for you, I can tell you that I've been getting together a little anthology, and I was sort of counting on using your poem 'Moshe Dayan's Other Eye'—"

"I wouldn't let you print that poem if you gave me ten grand," Gold said fiercely.

"The fee was fifty dollars," said Parsons. He strode to the kitchen; before Mrs. Bloodworth could dry her hands on her apron Parsons took them both and shook them, thanking her for a delightful evening. He bade good night to Professor Bloodworth, and, still urging Bean to come and see him, left with a shaken Fuller.

Sumner Bean and Stanley Gold left the house together. It was four in the morning; they walked in the middle of the street. They did not speak; at one point, and without warning, Bean crooked his arm through Gold's the way a stiff old-time lover might. This was the way they walked to the hotel, silently, arm in arm, feeling frail, as poetry was. And when they went to their separate rooms they did not say good night, but bowed slightly, trying to smile. In his bed, Gold continued the poem he had put aside the previous evening at 6:30. At his undersized hotel desk, Bean fiddled with headed note-paper; he did not begin writing immediately, but a poem was arranging itself in his head. Bean's and Gold's were only two of the poems Bloodworth later claimed as the seminar's own. There were two more: "A Night Call on Miss Dickinson" and "Pizza—A Sonnet."

HAYSEED

▲▲▲▲▲▲▲▲▲▲▲▲▲▲▲▲▲▲▲▲▲▲▲▲▲▲▲▲

IRA HUBBEL WAS TALKING TO HIS TWO ATTENTIVE BOYS at the single pump of his Jenney station on the main street of Stockton Springs. They heard a car slowing down, but seeing it was Warren Root's new Chevy convertible, the two boys walked over to a stack of tires which, for a time, they kicked glancing back at their father and Root. And then they sauntered closer to the car and stood gaping in their beaked baseball caps and greasy overalls like two birds, trying to hear.

"Just up from Bangor this minute," Root was saying.

Ira looked into Root's reckless face from under the long visor of a faded green fisherman's cap on which a license was pinned. Ira's face was tanned, creased rather than wrinkled, and gave the impression of having been smoked and cured like a tobacco leaf. His alert eyes were a luminous blue and watched Root with the close curiosity of pity.

"Better check the water," said Ira. He motioned to one of the boys, who heard. The boy got a large watering can and carried it to the front of the car. He hoisted the hood.

"Same old damn town," said Root, looking across the main street. He shifted away from the steering wheel and

108

made a right angle of his arms, one extended across the top of the front seat, the other along the door. He hooked his thumbs and began drumming emphatically with his fingers.

"Ain't Bangor." Ira was squirting water in droplets from a Windex bottle onto the mud-speckled windshield.

"Leave that be, Ira. I'm going to wash the car soon's I get home."

"Never mind, Chub." Ira rubbed the windshield with a handful of squeaking chamois.

"Ain't Bangor is right," said Root, shaking his head. "Why they got a ritzy new hotel opened up there, with two or three bars and a big ballroom and what all. People come all the way down from Portland to have a gander at it."

Ira was silent, busy with the windshield. Then he said, "That so?"

"Picked me up some chicken wire at the feed store," said Root.

"Trunk wired down good?"

"Not too good. But it didn't flap open."

"That's a blessing," said Ira. He looked at the pump. "You wanted it full up?"

"I guess."

"It's full up now," said Ira. " That's five sixty."

Root gave Ira a ten-dollar bill.

"Expected you yesterday," said Ira, taking the bill.

"Gave myself an extra day," said Root. In reflection, he pulled on his nose.

"Myron says you wasn't at the boarding house," Ira said politely.

"Now how does Myron know that?"

"Tried to call you up last night. They said you wasn't there."

"Moved to the new one on Thursday," said Root. "The hotel I was telling you about. The boys that carry your bags got these funny little suits and say yes sir. I got sick of that Jesus boarding house."

"Myron didn't know."

"No, Myron didn't know," said Root. "And I'll tell you something else. Lavinia didn't know neither." Root grinned.

Ira looked at the ground, then said softly, "I'll get your change."

"Stoved-in front," said Hubbel's boy, slamming down the hood.

"Skunk," said Root. He measured with his hands. "'Bout yay big. I stove *him*!"

Root was outside the car, stretching, examining the dent on the grill, when Ira came back with the change. Ira counted it into Root's hand, pressing the coins, flattening the bills, saying, "Five sixty. And forty is six, and one is seven, and two is nine—"

"But I'll tell you something," said Root, closing his hand on the money, "they still haven't learned to shoot pool in Bangor, and that's the God's truth. How about a quick game?" Root rubbed his palms and nodded at the drugstore, where there was a pool table.

"Maybe later," said Ira.

"I'm all stiff with the driving," said Root. "Come on, Ira."

"Got to watch the station," said Ira.

"You got your two boys to watch your Christly gas station, Ira. Now get over and shoot a game with me."

Ira hitched up his pants and followed Root across the street.

A game was in progress, but the two players looked up and backed away from the table when Root and Ira entered the store. A man in an apron behind the soda fountain greeted Root solemnly.

"Hi, Wayne," said Root to the man in the apron. To the players he said, "You boys should be in school."

The boys put down their cues.

"That's okay," said Root. "I don't care if you play hooky. Used to do quite a bit of that myself, didn't I, Ira?"

"They're giving us the table," said Ira.

"Finish your Jesus game," said Root.

"You go ahead, Mr. Root," said one of the boys.

"I don't like to horn in," said Root.

Ira took a cue and began chalking it. Root did the same. The boys obligingly racked the balls and dusted chalk marks off the rails.

"Didn't know you two worked here," said Root, and

laughed. He spotted the cue ball and lined up his shot, then gently sent the cue ball into the triangular formation. It nicked a corner and came to rest an inch from the barely troubled formation.

"Don't leave me with much," said Ira. But instead of nudging the cue ball, he blasted, breaking the formation and spreading the balls all over the table.

"You want me to win," said Root.

Ira coughed.

"I'd like a drink," said Root, sinking a ball.

"It ain't three yet," said Ira.

"I'd like a drink. Here," Root said to one of the boys, "go get us half a pint of vodka next door. Tell them who it's for."

The game proceeded quickly, Ira fumbling his shots, Root scoring often. The boy returned with the vodka.

"Oil up with Orloff's!" said Root. He knocked back two swallows, then gasped and wiped his mouth with the back of his hand. He passed the bottle to Ira.

Ira looked around the store before he drank; then he took a sip.

"Take a real slug," said Root. "Oil up, Ira!"

Ira tipped the bottle and took a mouthful. His eyes were watering when he handed it back to Root. He said, "Don't that stuff burn."

"First time I heard you complain about a free drink," said Root.

"I'm not complaining, Chub," Ira said quickly. "I appreciate it."

"Then have another one," said Root. He lined up a new shot.

"I'm seeing spots," said Ira. He screwed the cap onto the bottle.

Root said, "Son of a whore. That was an easy one."

One of the boys came forward and held the pool chalk out to Root. "Thank *you*," said Root, and smiled at the boy. The boy crept back to the raised bench and sat down.

As Ira was taking his next shot the door flew open with a bang and a man came in. He was heavy, rawboned, wearing a torn felt hat and overalls dusted with yellow chicken meal. He saw Root and closed the door carefully, turning the knob and making no sound. He said, "Sorry," and squinted, then bought some cough drops, nodded respectfully toward Root and, easing the door open, slipped out.

"What's he tiptoeing around for?" said Root. He rested the pool cue on his thumb and whacked a ball into a corner pocket. "I don't say this is the grandest town, but people treat you right."

"Yep," said Ira.

"Bangor's a waste from that point of view. Mighty unfriendly—reminds me of the navy, Bangor does. Those crazy Indians come up from Stillwater. Oh, they're a tough bunch when they get a little Orloff's in them. Look at you with them big square faces. I saw a hell of a fight a few nights back."

"Don't get down Bangor way very often," said Ira.

"It's a good experience," said Root, watching the table. "Like the navy. We'll go down there together next time, what do you say?"

"I'd like that, Chub."

Root grinned. "Might even get laid, eh? What would your old woman say to that?"

Ira cleared his throat and looked around. He grasped his pool with two hands. One of the high school boys was smiling.

"You mind your own business, sonny," said Root.

"Sorry, sir," said the boy.

The next time Root looked over both boys had gone.

"Have another swig, Ira. It won't kill you."

"Chub, I don't think—"

"Ira."

"I think I'll just have a bottle of tonic," said Ira.

"Put some of this into it," said Root. He showed the vodka.

"All right," said Ira. He smiled while Root splashed some vodka into his glass of orangeade. But he did not drink. He set the glass down on the raised bench.

"I can finish this game in three shots," said Root. He walked around the table, then began knocking the balls into the pockets. The balls dropped in three gulps. Root said, "How about another? You gave me that one, didn't you?"

"No, no," said Ira. "I'd better scoot back to the station."

"Another game wouldn't hurt." Root looked at his watch. "Half-past three," he said. "Bet Lavinia's tearing her hair."

Ira didn't move.

Root giggled. "She'll bust a gut when I get back, so I'm in no hurry. Women," he said, facing Ira, "they're so damn contrary, ain't they?"

Ira flicked his head up and down. "Sure are," he said. He glanced at Wayne, the man behind the soda fountain. At the glance, Wayne picked up a coffee cup and started to wipe it.

"You know what I always say, Ira?" Root held up the vodka bottle, saw there was still an inch left, and took a long pull. "I always say: You can't live *with* 'em, and you can't live with*out* 'em. And frankly, Ira, I know what the hell I'm talking about."

"You do, Chub. A good woman—"

"Ain't no such animal!" said Root. He laughed and drank again. "Now my name's Warren, as you know, and that's the name I use in Bangor."

"Warren," said Ira.

"Know what they call me? Take a guess."

"Can't guess," said Ira.

"I'll tell you. It's Don Warren—like Don Juan. Get it?"

"Oh, I see," said Ira.

Root shook his head and said, "Jesus."

"I'd better scoot back to the station," said Ira.

"You do that." But as Ira was leaving, Root called, "Ira, wait!" startling the old man. Root pointed to the glass of orangeade on the bench. "You forgot your drink, Ira. Set down and finish it."

Ira picked up the glass and drank it down with his eyes closed. He left, coughing.

"He's a funny old hayseed," said Root. "Ain't that right, Wayne?"

"Yes, sir," said Wayne, and began to blink and sniff in a rabbity way.

* * *

One of Ira Hubbel's boys was standing near the convertible. "I washed your car, Mr. Root."

"Much obliged," said Root. He tried to give the boy a tip. The boy refused it. "Groceries," said Root.

At Mason's, the grocery store, Root took a wire carriage and wheeled it around, filling it with cans. Harold Mason was at the cash register. Root said, "No cartons of Luckies."

"Aren't there any on the shelf, Mr. Root?"

"Not a one."

"Must be in the stockroom. I'll get you a carton."

"That's all right. I'll be back later."

"I won't be a minute," said Mason, hurrying to the back of the store.

"Didn't mean to cause him any bother," said Root to a woman holding a child. The woman, gawking by the door, seemed surprised that Root should address her. Root smiled. The woman turned away and left the store.

"Here you are," said Mason. "One carton of Luckies."

"Didn't mean to cause any bother," said Root.

"No bother at all."

"What's the bad news?"

"Pardon?" Mason looked shocked.

"The bill. How much do I owe you?"

"You don't have to pay now," said Mason. "You must have your hands full."

Root smiled. "I don't have an account here, do I?"

"No, you don't. But—"

"So how can I put it on account if I don't *have* an account? You tell me." Root looked around for a witness. He saw no one except Mason's wife, watching from the frozen-food section at the rear of the store.

"Suit yourself," said Mason. He added the column of figures on the paper bag, then rang up the amount on the clanking cash register. "That will be nine dollars and forty-eight cents."

Root paid and started to leave.

"Mr. Root?"

Root turned.

"I'm very sorry," said Mason, and he did not take his eyes from Root's.

Root shrugged and went out to his car.

The Root farm was just outside town, on a slope, at the end of a stony, rain-eroded driveway. Root put the car into second and drove casually, holding a knob attached to the steering wheel, spinning it slightly as the car slid sideways on the gravel and shuddered and jounced to the front of the house. He was out of the car and reaching into the back seat for the bag of groceries; drunk, he spoke his thoughts: "Hell with it. I bought them, she can lug them in."

Inside the house he called, "Lavinia! I'm back!" And again, "Lavinia!" sharply.

There was no reply and not even much of an echo. The doors were open all the way out to the sunlight on a sawhorse at the back. A plump, reddish chicken bustled mechanically, as if it ran on a spring, and pecked at the floor just inside the kitchen. Root turned and looked back at the car, then at the driveway. At his split-rail fence, which bordered the road, some children stood and were staring up at him. He went to shoo the chicken, but he did not go all the way to the kitchen, for halfway down the hall the sound of his own feet stopped him. He called his wife's name again, now softly, nearly a question; and then he took a sip of air and held it in his mouth.

Later, upstairs, he found the severed length of rope, the note, the overturned stool.

THE SOUTH MALAYSIA
PINEAPPLE GROWER'S
ASSOCIATION

▬▬▬▬▬▬▬▬▬▬▬▬▬▬▬▬▬▬▬▬

THEY HAD A DRAMA SOCIETY, BUT IT WAS NOT CALLED
the South Malaysia Growers' Drama Society; it was the
Footlighters, it met on Wednesday evenings in the club
lounge, and the Official Patron was the Sultan. He seldom
came to the plays and never to the club. It was just as
well, the Footlighters said; when the Sultan was at the
theater you couldn't drink at the bar between the acts,
which was why most of the audience came, the men anyway; and Angela Miller, who drove down from Layang
Layang every *The South Malaysia Pineapple Growers'
Association* Wednesday, said the Sultan was a frightful
old bore whose single interest was polo.

An effortless deep-voiced woman, much more handsome at forty-five than she had been pretty at twenty,
Angela had played a Wilde heroine six years before—that
was in Kota Bharu—and found the role so aggreeable, so
suited to her temper, that in moments of stress she became
that heroine; telling a story, she used the heroine's in-
flections and certain facial expressions, especially incredulity. Often, it allowed her to manage her anger.

It was Angela who told the story about Jan's first visit
to the club. Jan had looked at the photographs on the wall

116

of the bar and then sat in a lounge chair sipping her gimlet while other members talked. Only Angela had seen Jan rush to the window and exclaim, "What a *lovely* time of day!"

"All I could see were the tennis courts," said Angela later, "but little Jan said, 'Look at the air—it's like *silk*.'"

Jan was new, not only to the club and the Footlighters, but to Klang, where her husband had just been posted to cut down a rubber estate and oversee the planting of the oil palms.

"Anyone," said Angela, "who spends that long looking out the window *has* to be new Klang. *I* look and don't see a blessed thing!"

It had happened only the previous week. Already it was one of Angela's stories; she had a story to explain the behavior of every Footlighter and, it was said, every planter family. That exclamation at sundown was all the Footlighters knew of Jan on the evening they met to pick a new play. She was a pale young girl, perhaps twenty-six, with a small head and a very young baby. Some of the male Footlighters had spoken to Jan's husband; they had found him hearty, with possibilities backstage, but mainly interested in fishing.

Angela was chairing the meeting; they had narrowed the selection to *Private Lives* and *The World of Suzie Wong*, and before anyone asked her opinion, Jan said, "We did *Private Lives* in Nigeria." It was an innocent remark, but Jan was slightly nervous and gave it a dogmatic edge, which surprised the rest into silence.

"Oh, really?" said Angela in her intimidating bass after a pause. She trilled the *r* as she would have done on stage, and she glared at Jan.

"Yes, um," said Jan. "I played Amanda. Bill helped with the sets." She smiled and closed her eyes, remembering. "What a night that was. It rained absolute *buckets*."

"Maybe we should put it on here," said Duff Gillespie. "We need some rain over at my place."

Everyone laughed, Angela loudest of all. And Jan said earnestly, "It's a very witty play. Two excellent women's parts and lots of good lines."

"Epicene," said Tony Evans, pronouncing it *eppy-seen*.

"I've noticed," said Henry Eliot, a white-haired man who usually played fathers, "that when you use a big word, Tony, you never put it in a sentence. It's rather cowardly."

"That's who we're talking about," said Tony, affecting rather than speaking in the Welsh accent that was natural to him. "Noel Coward."

"Too-shay," said Duff, "pardon my French."

Jan had looked from face to face; she wondered whether they were making fun of her.

"That settles it," said Angela. "*Suzie Wong* it is."

"When did we decide that?" asked Henry, making a face.

"You didn't," said Angela, "*I* did. We can't have squabbles." She smiled at Jan. "You'll find me fantastically dictatorial, my dear. Pass me that script, would you, darling?" Angela took the gray booklet that Tony Evans had been flapping through. She put it on the table, opened it decisively to "Cast, in Order of Their Appearance," and ran the heel of her hand down the fold, flattening it. She said, "Now for the cast."

At eleven-thirty, all the main parts had been allotted. "Except one," said Jan.

"I beg your pardon," said Angela.

"I mean, it's all set, isn't it? Except that we haven't"— she looked at the others—"we haven't decided the biggest part, have we?"

Angela gave Jan her look of incredulity. She did it effectively, and it made Jan pause and know she had said something wrong. So Jan laughed, it was a nervous laugh, and she said, "I mean, who's Suzie?"

"Who indeed?" said Henry in an Irish brogue. He took his pipe out of his mouth to chuckle; then he returned the pipe and the chuckling stopped. He derived an unusual joy from watching two women disagree. His smile was like triumph.

"You've got your part," said Angela, losing control of her accent. "I should say it's a jolly good one."

"Oh, I know that! But I was wondering about—" Jan

looked at the table. She said, "I take it you're going to play Suzie."

"Unless anyone has any serious objections," said Angela. No one said a word. Angela addressed her question to Jan, "Do *you* have any serious objections?"

"Well, not *serious* objections," said Jan, trying to sound good-humored.

"Maybe she thinks—" Duff started.

Angela interrupted, "Perhaps I'm too old for the part, Jan, is that what you're trying to say?"

"God, not that," said Jan, becoming discomposed. "Honestly, Angela I think you're perfect for it, really I do."

"What is it then?"

Jan seemed reluctant to begin, but she had gone too far to withdraw. Her hands were clasping in her lap now she was speaking to Duff, whose face was the most sympathetic. "I don't want to make this sound like an objection, but the point is, Suzie is supposed to be well, *Chinese* . . . and, Angela, you're not, um, Chinese. Are you?"

"Not as far as I know," said Angela, raising a laugh. The laughter subsided. "But I *am* an actress."

"I know that," said Jan, "and I'm dead sure you'd do a marvelous Suzie." Jan became eager. "I'm terribly excited about this production, really I am. But what if we got a Chinese girl from town to play Suzie? I mean, a *real* Chinese girl, with one of those dresses slit up the side and that long black hair and that sort of slinky—"

Angela's glare prevented Jan from going any further.

"It's a challenging role," said Angela, switching her expression to one of keen interest. "But so are they all, and we mustn't weaken. Henry is going to play the old Chinese man. Would you prefer that Stanley did it?"

Stanley Chee, a man of sixty, with gold-rimmed glasses, was the Head Boy of the club, and at that moment he could be seen—all heads turned—through the bar door, looking furtive as he wiped a bottle.

Jan shook her head.

"It's going to be a hard grind," said Angela, and she smiled. "But that's what acting is. Being someone else. Completely. That's what I tell all the new people."

A DEED WITHOUT A NAME

▲▲▲▲▲▲▲▲▲▲▲▲▲▲▲▲▲▲▲▲▲▲▲▲▲▲▲▲▲

WE HAVE KNOWN THE CROWLEYS EVER SINCE WE AR-
rived in Singapore, and to be honest neither Harry nor I
found it the least bit strange that they should ring us up
in the middle of the night to tell us about that horrid ship
disaster in the harbor. It was only later that Harry said
he had had a few inklings all along, that it was "just like
the Crowleys," but that from practically every point of
view it was (as he put it) "very strange indeed," which
I take to mean he agrees with me.

Both Les and Beth—or as I now think of them, Lester
and Elizabeth—fancied themselves amateur detectives,
better than the fictional ones. At first there was not a bit
of this. He puffed his pipe and talked about meerschaum
and dottle and Turkish mixtures; and she was frightfully
women's pagy, with black stockings and eye make-up and
funny beads. He wore a medallion around his neck which
embarrassed Harry, though he said he had been wearing
it a lot longer than the youngsters these days, and she
said the same about her get-up. I shall never know how
they got away with it in London just after the war, a trying
time for us all; they could have got away with it in Hamp-
stead or Chelsea, I suppose, but certainly not in Sutton

where they claimed they had a maisonette. The boring thing about people who dress in this odd way is that they do so to invite comment and challenge approval, like children in company saying to their parents "I hope you die." They made Harry's life a misery simply because he always wore a cricketing tie, and Harry worked jolly hard as treasurer of the club. He earned that tie, but I'll never know where they earned the right to dress like an updated incubus, and succubus, who might be known to their friends as Inky and Sucky. And they always said my frocks were *infra*.

I was saying about the Crowleys and their detective stories. This subject came up one evening when I told her how thrilled I had been by *The Mousetrap* and had they seen it? She held a sip of sherry in her mouth and tasted it with a tight little smile. She swallowed; the smile was gone. "Did you hear that?" she called to Lester. "Yes," he said, and getting terribly excited he turned to me and said, "I thought it was such a lot of—"

Do people *have* to talk that way?

Ellery Queen was going off, they said. And Poirot ("with his mon doos and sacra bloos") was already beyond the pale. "The only writer worth mentioning is Simenon in the original," she said, though "mon doo" I shouldn't think recommended her as much of a French scholar. As I look back on Elizabeth and her nastiness and her French novels I always suspect that her great pleasure must have been in cutting the pages with some ever-so-interesting Oriental dagger. "And Doyle at his best," said Lester, "and B____ and Gr____." (These last two names, which he mumbled, were unfamiliar to me: I am positive that is why he said them.)

"You see, to have a proper murder story there has to be real sense of sin," she said.

A sense of sin! Well, that's the Crowleys all over. *The Mousetrap*, a diverting little gem by the mistress of the genre, didn't have a sense of sin, was that it? I remember the evening Harry and I saw it; I can imagine how it would have been spoiled for us if the Crowleys had been in the next stall and got all shirty about this gripping play not having a sense of sin. And neither will I repeat the uncharitable, not to say the beastly things the Crowleys said about Dame Margaret Rutherford.

I hold no brief for detective stories. Usually I find them very gloomy and always I find them badly written. I suppose Harry and I defended Agatha Christie and Arthur Conan Doyle because the Crowleys were being such awful bores. I get no joy from murder, though I admit some do, but in the normal way I would not have lifted a finger to defend a writer of crime fiction, except from an onslaught of prigs. I would cheerfully defend anyone in the same way—it is my nature—unless it was another prig. Elizabeth, I hope you and Lester can hear me.

Their infatuation was with murder stories of quite a different stripe. I have already admitted that I did not catch the names of the writers Lester mentioned, but when people say, "Oh, you know who I mean—I'm sure you must have heard of him," you can be fairly certain they know you haven't any idea who they mean. But I can well imagine what sort of stories the Crowleys liked. I had some indication of their tastes when they confessed that they too had thought of being murder-story writers. This is the chief characteristic of people who read rubbishy books; they take a shameless comfort in the fact that in a pinch they could quite easily duplicate them. Readers of murder stories are the biggest offenders here. I doubt that there is one of them who has not thought of setting pen to paper and dashing off a shilling shocker of his own. These aficionados of gore never actually write their stories, though they insist that with a typewriter and a bank holiday they would "type it up" (writing, for them, being something like crocheting a doily) and it would be a best seller. Sheer bloody-mindedness prevents them from ever attempting it; they much prefer telling it, with pauses, putting finger to lips and saying um-um, holding a roomful of people captive with boredom. Lester and Elizabeth did this all the time, they were forever going on about their "own story," interrupting each other to add bloody minutiae and getting terribly excited about what were (to me, at any rate, and Harry) rather dreary little mysteries with obvious clues, intended only to shock. I have no doubt that there was a sense of sin in *theirs*!

But their infatuation was with murder stories of quite a different stripe. For Lester and Elizabeth, the crime was everything and solving it did not worry them for a moment; in fact, the crimes they concocted were seldom solved at all. Their theory, I suppose, was that not all crimes are solved—that is, the best ones aren't. Their shockers took ages to tell and always had the servant in a terrible state (Ah Ho doesn't live in this compound and has to be driven home when the guests leave; Harry used to be furious and it always rained). A typical Crowley shocker was about a murder trial in which all the jury, the magistrate, the entire prosecution—everyone in the courtroom except the accused—was guilty of the crime. Of course the poor chap was found guilty and later gassed. (Was it that old gray-haired judge with a nose so big "it seemed," Lester put in, "as if he was perpetually eating a banana" who dreamed up that mess? I forget.) Here the point was that the honest man has no business in society: society is evil and will kill him. For the Crowleys there was no such thing as a good sleuth and no one was innocent except the accused, no one guilty except the law; I think that was how it went, and there was an awful lot of torturing. Positively diabolical.

I do not mean to suggest that the Crowleys were cruel to us or hurt us in any way, or for that matter that they were not, underneath it all, decent people in many ways. Her soufflés and his imitation of a West Country rustic (I can still hear him saying, "Ur, it bain't very furr...") did more than make up for their rather childish insistence on ticking off the writers of detective stories and their championing of the two I suppose infinitely more tiresome and bloodthirsty writers whose names were lost in the nimbus of Turkish tobacco smoke which hung between Lester's lips and my ear; I mean, B____ and Gr____. Perhaps it was the amusing working-class accent which Lester adopted when speaking about very serious subjects. (The middle class often use such devices as a cover for their embarrassment.) And the Crowleys, for all their admitted kinks and quirks, had excellent taste in antiques, little ikons and altars, maps and occult charts which fascinated Harry, who has been looking into old atlases ever since he heard of their annual appreciation of 10 per cent—a good deal sounder than most British investments, which are a scandal. They had cute little black drapes fitted across Lester's "meditation room" and inside very interesting snapshots of a bald and bug-eyed gentleman Lester said was his father. "A beastly man, a beastly man," Lester would say, and this for a reason I cannot guess at sent both Lester and Elizabeth into gales of laughter. They had such things as tiger skins and opium pipes, fascinating Oriental pots, and bric-a-brac imprinted with abracadabra. It was all, Lester said, his father's.

"Your father must have been quite a character," I said to Lester on one occasion. Harry and Elizabeth were in another room sampling a sort of rice dumpling very popular here with the Chinese.

"Oh, he was," said Lester, and with that he brushed his hand neatly across the curve of my bottom, so neatly that I could not accuse him of getting fresh, barely comprehending what he had done to me. I thought at the time that it was a skirt pleat freeing itself and touching me softly. I know better now. He never spoke again about his father, nor did I ask.

Our relationship, because it was not a relationship at all but rather an awareness of each other, had a forced heartiness about it and a bonhomie (how Elizabeth made a shambles of the pronounciation of this simple French word!) that was impossible to suppress. We were not good friends of the Crowleys' and never had been; this resulted in an uncertain distance which compelled us to do more for them than their best friends would have done, though God only knows who or where their best friends were. It is easier to say no to a friend than to one of these fumbling strangers; I much prefer the honesty of friendship, so does Harry. One is always doing something one finds unpleasantly intimate with someone one barely knows. It is always the way and it is the reason Harry and I make a point of "screwing our courage to the sticking place," so to speak, and getting to know people really well. As we have no children (Harry has a low "count") this is usually quite simple. We tried with the Crowleys but it never worked: we were always the new visitors, obliging them with kindnesses and remembering not to interrupt or offend either of them, and often going out of our way for them, always an inconvenience. Harry is such a dreadful sleeper; I remember how they used to urge us to stay on and dope Harry with coffee. We could not say no. We only said no once to the Crowleys, and that was the last time we saw them, when our so-called friendship ended; and this happened shortly after the incident I intend to tell you about right now.

It was near midnight when they rang. I know that because Harry was soaking his teeth, and he never does that before midnight. It is a small but useful courtesy he has practiced throughout our marriage and I am grateful to him for it. It is my luck that I have been blessed with very strong teeth and let me note here that Lester, although of Irish stock, had an unexpectedly fine set of teeth which he said were all his own. "That," I ribbed him, "comes of a long residence in England. In Ireland they'd be rotted to stumps!" Lester did not, happily for me, take offense at my harpish dig.

They spoke of two separate items when they rang and they did this in a rather clever way. Lester spoke to Harry first and told him of the ship disaster in the harbor. Apparently a tanker approaching the harbor spied another tanker just leaving. They were in the deep channel, near the islands called the Sisters, that leads to Collyer Quay. The approaching tanker signaled the other (two short blasts) to turn off. But it was early morning and the captain who had signaled had the impression he had not been heard, and so shortly after gave two more strong blasts on his whistle, or whatever it is they signal with on tankers. Here destiny dealt another card. Two short blasts means "turn to port" (left) but four short blasts means "turn to starboard" (right). The second tanker turned to starboard, was rammed amidships and sank in seventeen minutes, just long enough for four wild Chinese to find life jackets and leap to safety. The rest perished, the Scots captain and thirty of the crew. As for the other tanker, the one that had done all the signaling and ramming; well, that tanker steamed out to sea and was last heard of in Japan where it discharged its entire crew, including its (Liberian) captain. It suffered a bit of damage in the bow (front). A tragic tale, and one worthy of a Humphrey Bogart film if not a Joseph Conrad novel.

Then Elizabeth spoke to me. Were we interested in getting up a swimming party? I said an emphatic yes. One is able to see a great deal of one another on a swimming trip; there is candid revelation in seminakedness. We fixed it for the following Sunday and I said I'd bring sandwiches and my own liver pâté if they could be responsible for fruit and drink (I hinted at a jug of simple orange squash so that they would not feel obligated to hump a crate of beer). I was beside myself when I rang off.

Harry was pale. He told me what Lester had said about the ship disaster and added, "I fancy the poor blokes didn't have a chance." Poor *blokes*, you see; it sounds frightfully low, and Harry's father was a bishop. But I have said somewhere above that the middle class often uses working-class language when the thought expressed is unbearably serious. Harry, you are forgiven for this. I understand.

Then I told Harry what Elizabeth had said to me about swimming. Harry said fine, "as long as it isn't near the Sisters," and he tried a charmless laugh.

The scene at the Jardine Steps where we booked our motor launch was so picturesque: sampans and fisherfolk here, smugglers in undervests there, mothers giving suck to their round-cheeked kids on the quayside, and over there a foursome of RAF hearties with goggles and flippers setting out for a day of snorkling in the Straits! Much as I would like to linger here on the steps and allow a thorough consideration of the colorful comings and goings, I feel I must press on. Landscape is all very well, and there is much to say of the quaint splendor of these "pampered jades of Asia," but for my present purpose I am afraid it would only delay the telling of what is a far more important (to me, at any rate) if less pretty story.

Leaning against the gunwales (sides) of the launch as we putt-putted out into the harbor, I realized that we were not headed in the direction of Pulau Blakang Mati—where the bathing facilities are excellent and "the water is like ginger beer" in the unambitious simile of one of the local poets—but for the Sisters. These two heaps of stones, topped with stunted cacti and patient pitcher plants, loomed up in the channel of swirling water. And behind them, the low blue *blancmange* of Indonesia.

The two druids sat inside, leafing through the Sunday papers and smiling to themselves. Harry, poor Harry, tried to strike up a conversation with the Chinese pilot. The unmuffled engine roared, Harry shouted, the pilot replied in clacking Cantonese. The pilot's small daughter had come along, though for no more sinister reason than the daughter of the *Hesperus'* captain: "To bear him company." She stared in an intensely embarrassing way at Harry, who does not know a word of Cantonese but talks a great deal when he is upset.

I put on a brave face. I was not going to let the Crowleys know they had succeeded in spoiling what could have been quite a pleasant swimming party. But though my expression did not betray my alarm, I searched the water anxiously for the wreck of the tanker and thought at one point that just beneath the surface I saw the funnel (chimney) of the sunken ship. It turned out to be a rotten basket astir with seaweed.

The pilot communicated to us by means of clever wrist play and a series of little grunts that the tide was down and that he would have to drop anchor there while we swam ashore to the Sisters. This was agreed upon. There was no need for an elaborate change of clothes as we were wearing our bathing costumes under our street things. We folded our slacks and jumpers and dived into the channel and made for the shore, the Crowleys with morbid slowness, Harry and I thrashing desperately.

I felt the tug of the ripping tide on my arms, the slimy uprooted loofahs brushing my knees, and I thought with horror of the ghostly hulk which lay—who knew how close? The Crowleys probably did—beneath me, manned by the corpses of thirty Chinese and one valiant Scot. I have no idea how I made it to shore, but I did, and so did Harry. How ironic that the sun should beat down on us, that the sky should be so impossibly blue! A blasted heath would have been more appropriate, especially as in trendy bathing costumes the Crowleys crawled up the beach.

It was clear that both of them wished to raise the subject

of the tanker, for they remarked on the rainbows of oil
slick that slapped in the shallows. "Must be from our
launch," said Harry, who is nobody's fool and certainly
knew better than that. They also spoke about the curious
shadows in the water, and Lester said in that pompously
knowledgeable way of his: "Modern science really hasn't
a clue what goes on under the sea."

"Another one of your detective stories?" I remarked,
and I could tell it wounded him because he visibly winced
at me.

Seeing that they were getting nowhere, the Crowleys
then began telling Harry and I of something that had happened to them in I think Panama. The story does not bear
repeating; it is too horrible for that. But simply let me
say that it was about a stray dog they picked up, thinking
it was a worthy little animal. They fed it and cared for it;
it loved them and appeared perfectly docile. After a month
or two of care its coat was glossy and it showed tender-
ness, fetching sticks and wagging its tail. The family next
door, imitating the Crowleys' example, bought a small
puppy at a pet shop in the city. On seeing the puppy, the
Crowleys' hound leaped the hedge that divided the gardens and set upon the poor animal and tore it to pieces.
It turned out that the dog the Crowleys had befriended
was a "fighting dog" which is trained from birth to kill
other dogs, but is in all other respects quite normal. Apparently your Panamanian enjoys such sport and makes
bets on these dogfights in the same way as other savages
gamble on fighting cocks. I have told more of this story
than I had planned to. I don't have to say it chilled me
to the bone. And Lester had the impertinence to add,
"You see, there's a lesson in that."

The only lesson I could see was that one should be
careful in choosing one's friends, and I as much as told
him so.

We lunched on the launch. Another frantic swim. They
remarked politely on my cucumber sandwiches ("frail but
cooling") and ate all the pâté. Harry, who *will* let himself
be bullied, had their leavings. I made up for their gluttony
by having more than my share of wine (they did after all
bring a few bottles of a very acid Australian red). Harry,
sampling the wine, remarked, "It's a sincere little chap-

pie"—very much to the point, I thought. And then we dozed, eyed by the Chinese father and daughter from the stern (back).

Around three I suggested returning home, saying that the sun had given me a rather splitting headache and didn't they think enough was enough? They insisted on another swim; Harry refused to stand by me, he let himself be chivvied by them once again. We remained on board while the Crowleys floated on their backs and spat infantile little waterspouts into the air. "Thar she blows!" said Harry, but he ceased this when he detected an expression of severe reprimand on my face. It was at this point that, gazing off the side of the launch, I noticed a long and bejewelled snake slithering through the water, making its way amongst the rocks and coral. I did not call attention to it; even Harry was unaware of its existence (yes, dear). They are said to be quite poisonous and I thought then as I think now, that death can end an unsatisfying relationship as soon as rudeness, and I don't mind saying that I was hoping with all my heart that one or both of the Crowleys would sustain the fatal bite of that snake. It was not to be. Laughing absurdly they clambered into the launch and gave the pilot instructions for the voyage home.

Instead of taking the direct route back, we made what I thought was a pointless detour around St. John's Island, where the mental hospital is. It is also, at the south shore, the place where the channel meets the open sea, and consequently there is a terrific choppiness in the water. I was absolutely disgusted and decided to sun myself on the roof of the launch; but the pounding of the waves across the rocking bow of the launch was too much for me, and I realized that it was the express intention of the Crowleys to drown Harry and me, as they had signally failed to cow or frighten us. The sea hit and broke, hit and broke, setting the launch into an indescribable pitching, and tossing up bundles of lathered flotsam onto the foredeck.

And here, just south of that island madhouse, in the frothy sea, I looked up and saw that very strange thing. I peered at it for a long moment.

"Look at that," said Harry, who had also seen it. "Is it a lobster trap?"

Neither of the Crowleys spoke, though they watched it intently. On the cabin bench the small Chinese girl was peacefully, mercifully asleep.

It bobbed toward us, bloated to a grotesque buoyancy, very high in the water, rigid in the attitude of a resting swimmer.

"A sack of meal," said Harry.

We all watched it pass twenty yards off. It had limbs, but the hands were out of the water, and black, and clawing the air. It was much worse than seeing a corpse far off and deliberately averting your eyes. We did not take our eyes off it for a second! We pretended it wasn't human! Then it was too late: we knew we had been staring at a dead man for ten minutes or more.

The Chinese boatman threw his head back and laughed, for a corpse is considered unlucky, and it is by laughing hysterically that your Chinese reacts to mortal terror.

"You can't fool me," I said. "I know it's dead."

"No one is trying to fool you," said Lester. "But look—it's spinning so grandly."

The corpse wheeled around and around, like an inflated beach toy in a breeze.

"It *is* floating rather well," said Elizabeth, and she smiled: the lewd satisfaction of the torturer.

I closed my eyes and instantly wanted to kill them both. With my eyes shut I heard Harry say, "Quite possibly a fugitive bale of jute."

Poor Harry. That was no bale of jute. You knew what it was. But why didn't you say so then? Why did you wait until after we had paid the boatman and were home to agree with me? Don't you see that we could have confronted those two hellhounds with their beastliness? And why, whenever I bring this matter up, do you simply say that "we learned our lesson"?

As for me, I was brusque with the Crowleys. I remembered not to say cherrio but snapped a sharp good-bye into their faces. Harry will go on denying this, but I know pretty well what those arch bitches were up to, though I have not yet discovered the name for their deed, and without this word I cannot make a coherent accusation.

Harry keeps muttering that some people are intentionally devilish while others are plain crazy, and these days you don't know who to trust. This, as Harry knows perfectly well, explains nothing whatsoever. Now he refuses to discuss the matter and has talked repeatedly of leaving Singapore and taking me "for a long rest somewhere cool." If I do not know the name of what they did to us it is not because there is none. It is only a matter of time, and I have assured Harry that when I find out what it is I shall report all the findings which I have carefully noted here to the proper authorities.

YOU MAKE ME MAD

▲▲▲▲▲▲▲▲▲▲▲▲▲▲▲▲▲▲▲▲▲▲▲▲▲▲▲

"I THINK YOU'RE GOING COLORBLIND," SAID AMBROSE McCloud. Doris McCloud hitched herself forward to turn and stare at her husband. They had just pulled into their driveway and Doris was twisting the emergency brake when he took his pipe out of his mouth and spoke.

"I didn't want to mention it back there. Thought you might get rattled," said Mr. McCloud. He chuckled, a pitying kind of mirth, and said, "You went sailing right through two red lights. Scared the pants off me."

"You're imagining things, Ambrose," said Mrs. McCloud. But she did not sound convinced; her tone of voice contradicted what she said.

"Here," said Mr. McCloud, "feel my hand."

Mrs. McCloud took her husband's hand. "Why, it's gone all clammy!"

"You gave me a fright," said Mr. McCloud. "Back there."

"God," said Mrs. McCloud to herself, "I thought they were green."

"Better watch your step, Doris, or you'll rack yourself up," said Mr. McCloud. "Say what's on television?"

Mrs. McCloud didn't reply, not even when they were

in the house and sitting in front of the television set. Mr. McCloud filled his pipe; he did it methodically, packing it with his thumb and then brushing the little stringy droppings of tobacco on his shirt front back into his cracked plastic pouch. He was a man of sixty-three, two years younger than his wife. It was a difference in age she particularly resented, since he was very spry and chirpy and she was not. He was short, his gestures were precise; and he had a beautiful head of white hair which gave emphasis to his tanned face.

In the three months they had been in Singapore, Mr. McCloud had got the tan, and his healthy color was matched by a new vigor, the kind of rejuvenation that is promised to old people on the labels of patent medicine. During the same period his wife's face had grown waxen and she had begun to seem especially aged. It was as if, since coming to Singapore, she had learned feebleness, the way a younger woman might learn to put on airs. She shook, she forgot things and mislaid her shopping lists; she repeated herself and she had started that habit of the very old, of announcing what she was about to do: "Think I'll have a bite to eat . . . Time for my bath . . . Gosh, it's time I was in bed." She often accused her husband of making her that way, but still her doubt lingered to produce fear in her; the uncertainty was like being elderly and she had began to be afraid.

"I want to go home," she said finally.

"We've been through this one before."

"I mean it. Two old duffers like us shouldn't be living in a nasty place like this."

"*I'm* not an old duffer," said Mr. McCloud irritably. "Anyway, the company won't allow it. They'll probably keep me here until retirement, is what they'll probably do." Mr. McCloud thought a moment. "Not many younger fellers are interested in marketing plastics like I am."

"We should have rented an apartment in town," said Mrs. McCloud.

"They cost the earth," said Mr. McCloud. "What we save now we can spend later."

"Money," said Mrs. McCloud. "Your penny-pinching

makes me mad. Take the car. I think we're the only people in the world with an old Japanese car. You'd think we'd have a new one, as it's Japanese. But no. It's cheap, and what's cheap is dangerous."

"Some folks call it cheap," said Mr. McCloud. "And some—"

"I know what you're going to say," said Mrs. McCloud.

Mr. McCloud puffed his pipe. He said, "Lots of people would give their right arm to live in the country, instead of that noisy city. We're air-conditioned, no neighbors, lots of nice flowers, and it's quiet as—"

"Quiet as a grave," said Mrs. McCloud

"Well, that's what I was going to say."

Mrs. McCloud went reflective. "I was thinking about those lights," she said. "The ones I went through. What color were they, anyway?"

"Red," said Mr. McCloud. "I guess they looked like green to you. Take care when you pick me up tomorrow."

"Why, Doris," said Mr. McCloud the following afternoon. "You're all pale. you look like you've seen a ghost."

Mrs. McCloud was not sitting in the driver's seat. She shook her head and said, "You drive. I'm afraid."

"What the devil happened?"

"I almost crashed the car. The other man slammed on his brakes. He swore at me. I could hear him."

"What color was the light?"

"I don't know!" said Mrs. McCloud, and she looked as if she might cry.

"You're a bundle of nerves, Doris. I suggest we get a drink at that new hotel over on Orchard Road. What do you say?"

"That would be nice," said Mrs. McCloud.

Only the lower portion of the hotel was finished, the lobby, the cocktail lounge, and two floors for guests. The rest of the hotel, in various stages of completion, rose from this solid lighted foundation and seemed to disintegrate, from lighted windows, to a floor of glassless windows, to a floor of wall-less rooms, to brick piles and finally to a rickety structure of bamboo scaffolding at the top.

After two drinks, Mr. McCloud said, "I'll bet you could get a terrific view from the roof."

"Except," said Mrs. McCloud, "there's no roof. It's not up that far."

"I mean the top floor," said Mr. McCloud. "Bet we could sneak up there and get a really nice breeze and see the whole harbor."

Mr. McCloud seemed very eager, "Like a college boy," said his wife, which made them both smile.

"You go," said Mrs. McCloud. "I'll just park myself right here."

"Doris, you're no damned fun, you know that?" said Mr. McCloud. "To hear you talk anyone would think you're sixty-six years old."

"I *will* be," said Mrs. McCloud, "next March," and she started to cry.

"Aw, come on," said Mr. McCloud. "People are looking at you."

"I can't help it," said Mrs. McCloud. "Ambrose, you're so good and I'm such an old bag."

"You're as young as you feel," said Mr. McCloud, winking.

"I feel eighty-seven," said Mrs. McCloud.

"Let's skitter up to that top floor and have us a look, eh?"

"You know how I am about heights," said Mrs. Mc.Cloud. "I can't even climb a ladder to change a bulb. I go dizzy and feel limp as a rag." Her last phrase seemed to depress her and she cried again; many people in the coctail lounge turned to watch her.

Mr. McCloud dropped the subject and put his arm around his wife.

On the way home Mrs. McCloud said, "Ambrose, you just went through a red light!"

"Wrong again," said Mr. McCloud, driving fast. "It was green."

Mrs. McCloud stayed home for a week. She said it was a kind of convalescence, but instead of getting better she seemed to worsen, and each time Mr. McCloud came home his wife was paler and more feeble than she had been in the morning.

"I wish you'd come home for lunch," said Mrs. McCloud one day.

"I can get me a nice cheap lunch in town," said Mr. McCloud. "Little bowl of noodles, little bit of boiled fish, tasty little omelette." he lighted his pipe. "Sixty cents," he said, puffing.

"If you came home for lunch you could give me a hand when things go wrong."

"Don't tell me things have been going wrong, Doris."

"So many things," said Mrs. McCloud. "The other day it must have been something I ate. I think it was that sandwich you made for me, or it might have been a rotten egg, gave me tummy pains. I threw up. Today I blew a fuse. I just plugged in my hair dryer and it made a fizz and the TV shut off."

"Who fixed the fuse?"

"The gardener," said Mrs. McCloud.

"You didn't mention it when I called up."

"I was ashamed to," said Mrs. McCloud. "Thought I'd make you mad."

Mr. McCloud was looking at the hair dryer; it was pistol shaped and blackened. "She's all burned out inside. Wires must have shorted," he said. "Good thing you didn't get a shock," and he looked closely at his wife.

"I did," said Mrs. McCloud. "But it wasn't a bad one."

"That hair dryer cost a pretty penny," said Mr. McCloud.

"You can get a Japanese one to replace it."

"Not this month," said Mr. McCloud. "Oh, no! That'll have to wait, my dear. I can't be throwing my money away on hair dryers. I've got the insurance coming up and God knows what else."

"How will I dry my hair?" asked Mrs. McCloud.

"Sit in front of the air conditioner and shake your head," said Mr. McCloud gruffly. He stamped the floor with one foot, as he often did when he was very angry.

Several minutes of tuning, twisting the knobs with two hands, had produced only squawks, the underwater babble of Tamil, a high-pitched Chinese opera and some Malay gongs; though they came in clearly, the Chinese salesman said these foreign noises were not showing the radio to best advantage, and he became anxious. He apologized to Mr. McCloud and rearranged the antenna, whipping it around and just missing Mr. McCloud's left eye. Mr. McCloud touched at the lucky eye, making a light tear-wiping motion with his finger; but he was smiling.

The salesman offered to demonstrate a powerful short-wave radio.

Mr. McCloud said not to bother. "This one's going to do me just fine."

"Let me search some English," said the salesman breathlessly, still hunting. He flicked the antenna again.

Mr. McCloud leaned over and switched the radio off. He took out his wallet and grinned at the perspiring salesman. He asked, "How much?" He removed the pipe when he counted the money, licking his thumb and peeling the bills into the salesman's palm.

"That's a mighty fine little radio," said Mr. McCloud. "Get me some nice programs on that radio."

"Don't mention," said the salesman, smiling and opening the door. "See you next time."

That evening Mr. McCloud turned on all the air conditioners in the house. His wife complained, "I'm going to catch a death of cold," but Mr. McCloud calmed her saying, "Don't worry—I put them on low. Freshen up the room a bit," he said over the roaring of the air conditioners.

Mrs. McCloud said, "Time for my bath," and Mr. McCloud said, "You do that. I'll just sit here and fill my pipe."

Mrs. McCloud was singing softly to herself when Mr. McCloud entered the bathroom. She stopped singing and covered her breasts, holding one in each hand, as her husband, chuckling, turning the radio he carried in his hand onto full volume, said "Alley-oop" and pitched the yelling thing into the water at his wife's feet. He stepped quickly out and shut the door.

"*Ambrose!*" Mr. McCloud heard his wife scream. He nibbled on his pipe stem and smiled.

But she was out of the bathroom a minute later, wrapped in a towel and still wearing her plastic cap. "You silly old fool," she said, and slapped him with a force that sent his pipe flying out of his mouth.

Mr. McCloud did not retrieve the pipe. He watched his wife with the extreme attention of disbelief. She looked very angry, but not ill. At once, her face lighted with a thought, became concerned, grew rather small; she murmured, "Oh, God," and sat down, as if exhausted.

"Oh, shoot," said Mr. McCloud, and went to pack.

DOG DAYS

▲▲▲▲▲▲▲▲▲▲▲▲▲▲▲▲▲▲▲▲▲▲▲▲▲▲▲

THE INDIAN SAID: "I TAKE HAND OF WOMEN AND I squeeze and look in eyes, and if she return look and do not take hand away I know I can make intercourse. If also she squeeze my hand back it is most certain I can do it that very day. Only thing is, husband must be elsewhere."

He smiled and lifted his long brown hands, displaying their emptiness like a conjurer. He went on in his lilting voice: "In Asia, namely India, Pakistan, Indochina, Siam, here in Singapore, wherever, it is enough to touch body of woman, even arm or whatnot. If they do not object to that, path is quite open. And what," he inquired, "is done in States?"

"In the States?" Len Rowley thought a moment. "I don't know. I suppose we just come out and ask the girl if she wants to."

"Just looking and saying, 'Cheerio, let us make intercourse'?"

"No, probably something like, 'Would you care to come up for a drink?'"

"*A drink?*" The Indian threw his head back and gave

a dry croaking laugh. His teeth were bony and stained dark red with betel juice.

"Or to see your pictures. Any excuse really. The idea is to get her up to your room. If she says yes you know you can do it."

The Indian nodded and spoke to the empty chair beside him, solemnly rehearsing: "You would like to come up to take drink, yes?" Then he said to Len, "I think it is same as touching body. Woman enjoys, but she do not like to name."

That conversation had taken place in a bar on Serangoon Road, the heart of the Indian district of Singapore. Len had been out walking and had stopped at the bar. He hadn't intended to drink. But the Indian sitting by the door had given him a welcoming wobble of the head, and had smiled and tapped a chair seat and said, "Try some toddy?" They had talked, first about toddy, then about hot food, then about women. Len did not ask the Indian's name, nor did he ever see the Indian again.

But Len had replayed the Indian's voice many times. He found the explanation satisfying and revealing, such a close glimpse into the mind of Asia that he had never divulged it to anyone. It was like a treasure map, described by a casually met pirate and committed to memory. *I take hand of woman and I squeeze . . . It is enough to touch body*. The Indian had a way of saying *body*—he had pronounced it *bho-dhee*, speaking it with wet lips and heavy tongue-working—that made it sound the leering name for something vicious.

Len Rowley was a private soul, and marriage had increased his loneliness by violating his reveries. His attachment to Marian was not deep: he had lingered beside her for nearly seven years. She had put him through college, and now as an expatriate lecturer in English literature he was paying the bills. Marian was learning to play the guitar which hung on a hook in their living room. Friends found them an odd couple. Len and Marian talked of divorce, in company; this frightened listeners, but it always seemed to bring them together. Len was sometimes startled to recall that he had been unfaithful only once—with a prostitute in Newark, a year after the marriage. That was like making love to a chair tipped on its back and it cost Len twelve dollars.

The Forbeses and the Novaks were over for drinks. In a room full of people, Len became a recluse: he was still mentally speaking to the Indian.

But Ella Novak was saying, "In *Midnight Cowboy*, yes, that party. Remember? When Ratso faints? It was actually filmed at Andy Warhol's! That was a *real party*!"

"It's the new thing," Tom Forbes said. "Of course, your French have been doing it for years—at least Truffaut has."

Marian said, "Interesting, isn't it? Like Eldridge Cleaver's wife being in *Zabriskie Point*."

"Which one was she?" asked Ella in annoyance.

"At the beginning, when those students—I think they were students—were talking. With the hair. Holding the pencil and sort of . . . leading the discussion."

"Has anyone here seen *Easy Rider*?" Joan Forbes put in.

"That hasn't come to Singapore yet," said Ella.

"And probably won't," said Tony Novak. "Unless the Film Society gets it."

"Len still refuses to join," said Marian, looking at Len in the corner, slumped in the Malacca chair with a dreamy look in his eyes.

Roused, returned to the living room by Marian's words and the ensuing silence, Len said, "Film Society. Foreigners out of focus. Too much work reading all those subtitles!"

"I knew he was going to say that," said Marian to Tony. "He's really very puritanical."

Len smiled. He heard: *It is enough to touch body. Bhodhee.*

"Tom and I saw it when we were on leave," said Joan, adding, "*Easy Rider*."

"I didn't know you got home leave every year," said Marian.

"Ford Foundation," said Joan, and put her hands primly into her lap.

"We don't go home until seventy-two," said Marian. "Seventeen months more."

Tom Forbes asked Marian about Len's contract, and

he commiserated while Joan Forbes explained to Ella and Tony what happened in *Easy Rider*.

Len was silent. He heard the Indian's piratical voice and he watched the kitchen. Ah Meng was at the sideboard flexing a plastic freezer tray and popping the ice cubes into a pewter bucket. She stood in the bright rectangle of the half-open door, a shelf of corn flakes and Quaker Oats behind her head making her unremarkable profile more interesting. Her forehead was long and sloping, her pug nose set just below the rise of her high cheeks; her chin was small but definite, her mouth narrow and almost grim. Len could see her stiff black hair which was wound in a pile on her head, and he knew what her eyes were like: hooded, the sly changeless shape of the skeptic's; they were amused eyes, but some would say contemptuous. She was all but breastless and only her hands could be called beautiful, but it was the total effect that excited Len, the flower and stalk of face and body, the straightness of her length, her carriage. In a slim woman posture was beauty. She was tall for a Chinese and she moved in nervous strides like a deer.

Len had compared her with others' servants: the Forbeses' Ah Eng had muscular legs, bowed as a pair of nutcrackers. The Novak's Susan was a pale, pudgy, worried-looking little thing who always wore the same dress and once went bald. Tony was on the verge of firing her but, fortuitously, her hair grew back, porcupiny at first, then to her old bush.

When there was company, as on this evening, Ah Meng wore a loose blouse (raising to show a flat stomach when she reached for clean glasses on the top shelf), and tight, red skier's slacks. She went about the house swiftly, treading on the ankle loops of her slacks, in bare feet: Len found the feet attractive for the wildness they suggested. She had been with the Rowleys for nearly three months—replacing the bossy old Hakka woman—and for much of that time Len Rowley had been trying to get into bed with her.

Trying was perhaps the wrong word. He had been thinking constantly about it, the way he thought of the Indian's advice. But something a man at the university had said made him hesitate. It was in the Staff Club. A man from

Physics left, and Davies from Economics said, "See that bloke?" Davies told a story which cautioned by horrifying: the man from Physics had pinched his house girl's bottom. That very evening the girl disappeared, and the following day at a stoplight three youths jumped into the man's car, beat him with bearing scrapers, slashed him, and fled. The man still wore bandages. The house girl's boy friend was in a secret society, and the boy friend's final piece of revenge was upon the next girl the man employed. She was threatened; she resigned. This became known, and no one would work for the man. Davies said the man was going to break his contract and go home. That for a bottom-pinching.

This story had to be balanced against the easy explanation of the Indian; it made Len hesitate but he did not put the thought of sleeping with Ah Meng out of his mind. Sometimes he wondered why and decided it was lust's boldness, lechery's curiosity for the new. Unlike the man who feels challenged by the unwilling, Len was aroused by those who were passive, who would say yes instantly. He didn't like the devious ploys of love, and it was Ah Meng's obedience ("Shut the door" "Yes, mister") that made an affair seem possible.

For his lust he blamed his dog days. In some of the books he lectured on they were mentioned as days of excessive heat, unwholesome influences, practically malignant. The dog days were the hottest time of the year; the days Len passed, replaying the Indian's words and staring into the kitchen at Ah Meng were the hottest in his life. And it was literally true: it was always ninety in Singapore.

But hotter on Thursdays, Marian's Film Society night. These nights Len sat, soaking his shirt with sweat and wondering if he should make a move. Ah Meng would be in the downstairs shower, the one that adjoined her room, sluicing herself noisily with buckets of water and hawking and spitting. Later she would sit on the backstairs, holding her small transistor to her ear.

The story of the man in Physics restrained him; but there was something more. It was shame. It seemed like exploitation to sleep with your house girl. She might be frightened; she might submit out of panic. The shame created fear, and fear was an unusual thing: it made you a simpleton, it unmanned you, it turned you into a zombie. It was as a zombie that he had passed nearly three months.

". . . early class tomorrow," Tom Forbes was saying. He was in the center of Len's living room, stretching and yawning, thanking Marian for a lovely evening.

Len looked up and saw that everyone was standing, the Forbeses, the Novaks, Marian, waiting for him to rise and say good night. He leaped to his feet, and then bent slightly to conceal his tumescence.

"What's on?" asked Len, who was marking essays on the dining-room table. Marian clawed at objects inside her handbag.

"*Knife in the Water*," she said, still snatching at things inside the bag. She muttered, "Where are those car keys?"

"They usually show that one," said Len. "Or a Bergman."

"And some cartoons," said Marian, who hadn't heard what Len had said. "Czech ones," she said, looking up, dangling the car key.

"Enjoy yourself," said Len.

"I've told Ah Meng to heat the casserole. Tell her whether you want rice or potatoes." Patting her hair, snapping her handbag shut, Marian left the house.

As soon as Marian had gone Len pushed the essays aside and lit a cigarette. He thought about Ah Meng, the man in Physics, what the Indian had said. It occurred to him again—this was not a new perception—that the big mistake the man had made was in pinching the girl's bottom. That was rash. The Indian would have advised against it. There were subtler ways.

Ah Meng was beside him.

"Yes?" He swallowed. She was close enough to touch.

"Want set table."

"Okay, I'll take these papers upstairs. Make some rice." Distracted, he sounded gruff.

And upstairs at his desk, he continued to pursue his reverie. A squeezed hand was ambiguous and had to be blameless, but a pinched bottom signaled only one thing— and was probably offensive to a Chinese. Also: if Ah

Meng had a boy friend, where was he? She took a bus home on her day off. A boy friend would have picked her up on his motorbike, a secret society member in his car. The Indian's way seemed unanswerable: his method was Asian, bottom-pinching was not.

"Mister?" Ah Meng was at the study door. "Dinner."

Len got up quickly. Ah Meng was in the kitchen, scraping rice from the pot, by the time he had reached the second landing. He was breathless for a moment, and he realized as he gasped for air that he hurried in order to catch her on the stairs.

He ate, forking the food in with one hand and with the other retuning the radio each time the overseas station drifted off into static. He stared at the sauce bottles, and forked and fiddled with the radio knobs.

He put down his fork. It made a clank on the plate. Ah Meng was in the room, and now leaning over the table, gathering up silverware, piling plates, rolling up placemats. She said, "Coffee, mister?"

Len reached over and put his hand on hers. It was as sudden and unexpected as if his hand belonged to someone else. His hand froze hers. She looked at the wall. *I take hand of woman and I squeeze* . . . but the damned girl wouldn't look him in the eyes! It was getting awkward, so still squeezing he said, with casualness that was pure funk, "No, I don't think I'll have a coffee tonight. I think I will have—" He relaxed his grip. Her hand didn't move. He tapped her wrist lightly with his forefinger and said, "A whiskey. I think I'll have a whiskey upstairs."

Ah Meng turned and was gone. Len went upstairs to think; but it took no deep reflection for him to know that he had blundered. It had happened too fast: the speed queered it. She hadn't looked at him. He thought, I shouldn't have done it then. I shouldn't have done it at all.

Ah Meng did not bring the whiskey. She was in the shower below Len's study, hawking loudly. Spitting on me. He took his red ball point and, sighing, poised it over an essay. " 'The Canonization' is a poem written in indignation and impatience against those who censored Donne because of what is generally considered to have been his—"

Len pushed the essay (Sonny Poon's) away, threw down the ball point and put his head in his hands.

The front door slammed. The house was in silence.

This is the end, he told himself, and immediately he began thinking of where he might find another job. He saw a gang of Chinese boys carrying weapons, mobbing a street. He winced. An interviewer was saying, "Why exactly did you leave Singapore, Mr. Rowley?" He was on a plane. He was in a dirty city. He was in an airless subway, catching his cock on a turnstile's steel picket.

There was a chance (was it too much to hope for?) that she was just outside, on the back steps, holding her little transistor against her ear. He prayed it was so, and in those moments, leaving his study, he felt that strange fear-induced fever that killed all his desire.

He took the banister and prepared to descend the stairs. Ah Meng was halfway up, climbing purposefully, silently, on bare feet. There was a glass in her hand. She wore pajamas.

"I heard the door. I—"

"I lock," she said. She touched his hand and then bounced past him, into the spare bedroom. Len heard the bamboo window blind being released and heard it unroll with a flapping rattle and thump.

His first thought the next morning was that she had left during the night. Shame might have come to her, regret, an aftertaste of loathing. There was also the chance that she had gone to the police.

Len dressed hurriedly and went downstairs. Ah Meng was in the kitchen, dropping slices of toast into the toast rack as she had done every morning since the Hakka woman left. Marian took her place at the table across from Len and Ah Meng brought their eggs. Ah Meng did not look at him. But that meant nothing: she never did.

Marian chewed toast, spooned egg and stared fixedly at the corn-flakes box. That was habitual. She wasn't ignoring him deliberately. Everything seemed all right.

"How was the film?"

Marian shrugged. She said, "Russian film festival next month."

"Ivan the Terrible, Part One," said Len. He grinned.

But he could not relax. That girl in the kitchen. He had made love to her only hours before. Her climax was a forlorn cry of "Mister!" Afterward he had told her his name and helped her pronounce it.

"I thought you'd say something like that." Marian turned the corn-flakes box and read the side panel.

"Just kidding," said Len. "I might even go to that festival. I liked the Russian *Hamlet*."

"Members only," said Marian. She looked bored for a moment, then her gaze shifted to the tablecloth. "Where's your lunch?"

Every morning it was beside Len's plate, in a paper bag, two sandwiches with the crusts trimmed off, a banana, a hard-boiled egg, a tiny saltcellar, rambutans, or mangosteens if they were available at the stalls. Ah Meng, neat and attentive, made sharp creases in the bag, squaring it. The Staff Club food—maybe it was the monosodium gultamate?—gave him a headache and made him dizzy.

Today there was no lunch bag.

"Must be in the kitchen," said Len. "Ah Meng!"

There was no cry of "Mister?" There was no cry.

"I don't think she heard me," said Len. He gulped his coffee and went into the kitchen.

Ah Meng sat at the sideboard, sipping tea from a heavy mug. Her back was to him, her feet hooked on the rung of her stool.

"Ah Meng?"

She didn't turn. She swallowed. Len thought she was going to speak. She sipped again at her mug.

"My lunch. Where is it?"

She swallowed again, gargling loudly. That was her reply. It was as if she had said, "Get stuffed."

"Is it in the—" Len opened the refrigerator. The lunch was not inside. He was going to speak again, but thought better of it. Marian was around the corner, at the table—out of sight but probably listening. Len found a paper bag in drawer. He put three bananas in it and looked for something more. He saw a slice of bread on the sideboard and reached for it. Ah Meng snatched it up. She bit into it, and sipped at her mug. Her back seemed to wear an expression of triumph. Len left the kitchen creasing the bag.

"Got it," he said. He went behind Marian and kissed her on her ear. She was raising a spoonful of egg to her mouth, which was open. She stopped the spoon in midair, held it, let Len kiss, and then completed the interrupted movement of the spoon to her mouth.

That evening, when Len returned from the department, Marian said, "Ah Meng wants a raise."

"Really?" said Len. "I thought we just gave her one."

"We did. At least you were supposed to. I wouldn't put it past you to hold back the five dollars and buy something for yourself."

"No," said Len. He ignored the sarcasm. He *had* given Ah Meng the raise. He remembered that well: it was one of the times he had been about to seize and press her hand; but he had handed over the money and panicked and run. "I did give it to her. When was that? About a month ago?"

"I told her she gets more than the Novaks' Susan, and doesn't have children to mind. She gets her food and we pay her Central Provident Fund. I don't know what more she wants."

"What did she say?"

"She insisted. 'Want five dollar, *mem*,' " said Marian, imitating absurdly. Her mimicry was all the more unpleasant for the exaggerated malice of its ineptness. "It's not the five dollars, it's the principle of the thing. We gave her a raise a month ago. If we give in this time she'll ask again next month, I know. I told her to wait until you came home. You're better with her."

"Maybe we should give it to her," Len said. "Five bucks Singapore is only one sixty US."

"No, I expect you to be firm with her. No raise this month!"

In the kitchen, Ah Meng faced him—was that a sneer or a smile? Len said, "*Mem* says you want a raise. Is that right?"

She didn't blink. She continued to sneer, or perhaps smile. There was a red mark, just at the base of her neck, near the bump of her shoulder bone, a slight love scratch. From his own hand.

"Says you want five dollars more."

Her expression was that of a person looking at the sun or facing a high wind. It was a look only the Chinese could bring off. It revealed nothing by registering the implausible, severe pain. And this pain had to be discounted, for the face, on closer inspection, bore no expression at all: the eyes were simply a shape, they were not lighted, they gave Len no access.

Marian, out of sight, called from the dining room: "Tell her if she does her work properly we'll give her something around Christmas!"

"If you do your work properly," said Len loudly, taking out his wallet, fishing around and discovering that he had three tens and two ones, and then giving her a ten which she folded small and put in her handkerchief and tucked into the sleeve of her blouse, "—if you do your work properly we *might* give you something around Christmas. But we can't give you anything now."

The *might* came to him the spur of the moment, and Marian, who overheard, thanked him for it.

Len felt cold and started to shake. He went upstairs and clicked his red ball point at the unmarked essays. His dog days were over. But something new was beginning: intimidation. He didn't like it.

For the next few days he stayed up until Marian went to bed. Then he made his lunch in the kitchen, remembering to crease the paper bag, and this he placed on the dining room table, which was set for breakfast.

On Tuesday he had an idea. Marian was having her Pernod on the verandah, a touch she learned from a foreign film; she played with the small glass and watched its cloudy color.

"Is Ah Meng around?" Len whispered.

"At the market. We ran out of salt."

"Then I don't have to whisper." But this was a whisper. Len had downed five stengahs on the way home. "Marian, seriously, I think we should fire her."

"Why?" Marian frowned.

Len expected to be challenged, but not so quickly or (Marian was squinting at him) aggressively.

"Lots of reasons, "said Len, starting.

"I thought you were so pally with her."

"Me? Pally? That's a laugh." Len forced a laugh. He heard its cackling falsity as a truly horrible sound, and stopped. "Here, look what she did to my pants."

Len stood and showed Marian his leg. On the thigh was a brown mark of an iron, the shape of a rowboat. Between the Conrad lecture and the Donne tutorial Len had borrowed an iron from a Malay woman at the Junior Staff Quarters, and he had scorched his pants in his locked and darkened office. "Burned the hell out of them."

"That's a shame," said Marian.

"Burned the hell out of them," Len repeated.

Marian said, "You know, I've never said anything, but she's done that lots of times to my dresses. She scorches the collars."

"That's it then! Out she goes!"

"Okay, Len, if you say so, But there's going to be trouble with the Labor Exchange. It'll be just like the Novaks."

"What about the Novaks?"

"Investigated," said Marian. "By the Labor Exchange. After Susan's hair fell out, Tony said he didn't want to see her around, couldn't stand that bald head, or so he said. The Labor Exchange came to investigate—Susan told them of course—and there was a great to-do."

"I didn't know they did things like that."

"Went on for weeks," said Marian. The Pernod was to her lips.

Ah Meng entered the house and went into the kitchen.

"I'll speak to her," said Marian.

"That's okay. I will—they're my pants," said Len.

He went into the kitchen and closed the door. Ah Meng's back was to him; she was removing small parcels wrapped in newspaper bound with rubber bands from her market basket. Len made himself a gin and tonic.

"I guess we ran out of salt, eh?"

Ah Meng walked past him and closed the refrigerator door hard.

Len went out to the verandah.

"She says she's sorry.

Thursday came. Len asked, barely disguising the desperation in his voice, "Say Marian, how about letting me come with you to the Film Society. We can go out to eat afterward. What do you say?"

"Are you putting me on?"

"No, honest to God," said Len, his voice cracking. "Take me. I won't make any comments. I'd love to come."

"Mister is coming with me," said Marian to Ah Meng later.

Momentarily, Ah Meng faced a high wind; then she turned away.

The film was *L'Aventura*. Len watched with interest. He murmured that he was enjoying it, and he meant it. At the end, when Sandro sits abjectly on the bench and wrings his hands and starts to cry, blubbering with a pained look, Len understood, and he snuggled close to Marian in the darkness of the Cultural Center. Marian patted him on the knee. Afterward, as Len promised, they went to the Pavilion and he had cold, silky oysters with chili sauce, and tankards of stout.

Marian said, "We should do this more often," and at home, confidentially, "Keep me awake, Len," which was the whispered euphemism she used when she wanted to make love. Len was tired, but put the fan on full and made love to Marian with resolve, allowing his vigor to announce his new fidelity. Then he turned the fan down.

He lay on his back, his hands folded across his chest, proceeding feetfirst into sleep; but even much later, in the stillness of deep night, sleep was only to his knees. His eyes were open, his mouth clamped shut, and he was apprehensive, at that stage of fatigue where one's mind is vulnerable enough to suggestion to be prodded and alarmed and finally reawakened by a sequence of worrying images, broken promises, papers not marked, unpaid bills. He shooed his thoughts as they appeared tumbling and circling like moths attracted to the glowing bulb of his half-awake brain. He made an effort to switch off his mind—as one would a lamp in an upper room on a summer night, so as to quiet what had collected and not to attract more. But something in that darkness stung him: it was the thought of his lunch.

He went down to the kitchen. The sleepiness made him look like a granny in rumpled pajamas and electrified hair—like the elderly Hakka woman with the simian face and loose *sam foo*, her silk trousers with cuffs a yard wide, her narrow shoulders and square, swollen knuckles. He muttered like her and nodded at what he was doing, and just like her, in the curious conserving motion of the very old, fussed nimbly with his hands and at the same time shuffled slowly in broken shoes. He opened and closed cupboards, found a lunch bag, cut tomatoes, and he dealt out bread slices onto the sideboard as if starting a game of solitaire. With his impatient fingernail he pecked the boiling egg into its suds of froth.

A hand brushed the back of his neck. It was a caress, but he reacted as if dodging a dagger swipe.

"You scared the life—"

Ah Meng took his hand and did not let go. "Ren," she said, giving his name the rising intonation of a Chinese word.

Len shook his head. He said, "No."

Ah Meng pressed his hand. She was unhurried, looking at him without blinking. She tugged. Len tried to pull away. But she was the stronger; with his free hand Len turned the gas off under the cooking egg. She led him to her room. He would have time before dawn to finish making his lunch.

A BURIAL AT SURABAYA

▲▲▲▲▲▲▲▲▲▲▲▲▲▲▲▲▲▲▲▲▲▲▲▲▲▲▲▲▲▲▲

AFTER ABE SASSOON DIED IN TRETES, HIS COOK GOT A *jaga* to guard the house and then took a taxi to Surabaya to tell me. He chose me because my cook was related to him, and what he said was that Abe, normally an early riser—always in his vegetable gardens by six o'clock—was not up for breakfast that morning. The cook had forced the door and found Abe in bed clutching the mosquito netting he had yanked right off its pulley. It was draped in tangles over his face, giving the cook the impression he had smothered. I knew this couldn't be true. Abe had a bad heart.

I was having lunch at the time. The cook stood in the kitchen doorway, shouting the information, awkwardly trying to convey sorrow in his shrill parrot's voice. He said he came quickly because he knew we had to bury the old man before nightfall according to *Yehudi* custom. I thanked him for remembering that, gave him his taxi fare and told him to go back to the house and wait for us.

Hesitantly he asked for some "coffee money" for the *jaga*.

We have known better times, and I can recall when that cook would not have had to take a taxi to tell me.

153

We even had a synagogue in Malang—the rabbi there was a very learned fellow who always had his nose in a book. The telephones were better then, and you could pick it up and tell the operator the town you wanted and in minutes you would be gabbing away, clear as a bell. Now, the telephone squawks, then goes dead in your hand, and no one risks sending a cable. People will say it was when the Dutch left that things went to pot, but it wasn't: it was when the sugar prices fell. It doesn't matter now; there aren't enough Jews in Surabaya to support one synagogue, and business hasn't been good since the early fifties. Our age is an advantage. It means fewer interruptions—no marriages, no births. We don't observe the holidays, and it seems that every death over the past ten or fifteen years has happened after the person went to a hospital in Singapore. I can't say I looked forward to these deaths, but they gave me a chance to pick up a little stock for my business, which is mainly ship's hardware. I was thinking to myself, as I was driving over to Mr. Aaron's, that it would have been simpler for all of us if Abe had died in Singapore.

"I'm not surprised," Mr. Aaron said. But he had closed his eyes on hearing the news, and his wife had groaned. "We haven't seen Abe down here for months." He shook his head. "We should have visited him, you know. And the funny thing is, I passed through Tretes a week ago. It was so late I thought I'd better hurry back. My driver is hopeless after dark. I bought a basket of apples and didn't see anyone."

Mrs. Aaron was sitting next to her husband. Her plump shoulders shook with sobs, and when Mr. Aaron mentioned buying the apples and coming straight back she groaned again in what struck me as the deepest grief, disappointment.

"What time did it happen?" Mr. Aaron asked.

I had forgotten to ask the cook, but he had discovered him in the morning, so I guessed it was after midnight.

"Let's call it four A.M.," said Mr. Aaron. Mrs. Aaron looked at him and seemed slightly horrified; but she didn't say anything.

Mr. Aaron shrugged, not carelessly but hopelessly. "I was just going to have my nap," he said, pulling off his corduroy slippers and showing them to me.

"I thought we could use your van," I said.

"Oh, yes," he said, lacing his shoes. "Gunawan will be back about three. We can go up together. We'll have to leave the burial till tomorrow."

"Disgraceful," Mrs. Aaron said.

"We can't bury him any quicker than that," said her husband. "It's lucky he hasn't got a wife who'll see us doing it this way. That would be awful for her."

"It *is* awful," Mrs. Aaron said in a whisper more terrifying than a shout.

"It can't be helped," said Mr. Aaron. "Benjamin can conduct the ceremony. Is that cousin of Abe's still in Hong Kong, do you think?"

"Benjamin will know," I said.

"Try to calm yourself, Lool," said Mr. Aaron to his wife. "Get Benjamin on the phone and tell him about Abe. He can cable—what's the fellow's name? Greenman? Greenberg? We'll go around town and tell the people here. Everyone's going to be napping; its after two." He sighed. "I haven't finished my papaya."

Mrs. Aaron said, "What if it was you? That's what I keep thinking! I don't want it to be like this, to make a chore out of your funeral."

Mr. Aaron, like me, was born in Baghdad; but he looks like a man of the desert, and I have always looked like an ironmonger. His lean face has the furrows of dry soil, aging like erosion; he has a skinny hawk nose, his teeth are bad, black from cheroots and the poor food at Tjimahi Camp during the war. He often jokes, though he never smiles. He said to his wife, "At least, when I die no one will have to drive all the way to Tretes to pick up my body."

Glassman was the cousin's name. I remembered it as we were driving back in the van. None of us had ever seen him, but Abe had told us that if we were ever in Hong Kong we should look him up—he'd be glad to see us. Abe made a point of saying that this Glassman was something important in one of the banks there.

In the old days we might have seen him at a wedding, like the Meyer girl's in Djakarta. Old Meyer invited people from all over. They looked out of place—they kept saying how hot it was—and asked us how was business and why not try Manila or Singapore or wherever, if it's so bad? No one admitted it was bad, but these strangers knew the sugar price was down; and none of us said that Surabaya was hotter than Djakarta. You could look at people's shoes and know exactly how business was, and more than that, you could tell from their shoe styles where their business was. The Philippine friends had these huge pebbly-orange or purplish American shoes, the ones from Singapore and Hong Kong had English-style, rather smaller, without laces, and other people had low, narrow Italian ones with thin soles, bankers' shoes. Ours were old-fashioned, square toed and stitched, and some were scuffed from the train. We were staying with friends, not in hotels where the room boys polish them every night. It was quite a wedding, and after the champagne some of us sat up all night, liking the company, drinking cold little glasses of Bols geneva and eating beady caviar on small squares of toast. "I wish we could meet like this every year," said Meyer. "We've got enough money—we owe it to ourselves." He had enough money, but he went to Zurich a few years later, and they say his daughter's in Israel. The rest of us took our hangovers to Surabaya.

"Glassman wasn't at the Meyer wedding," I said to Benjamin the next day.

"Who says?" Benjamin is a sharp one, pretending to be a bit older than he actually is, because he knows he can have the last word that way. He uses an old man's preoccupied gestures, and looking thoughtful says as little as possible.

"I didn't see any Glassman there," I said. "And I'm sure I met everyone."

"He was there," said Benjamin.

"I didn't see him either," said Mr. Aaron. "I think you're making this up, Ben."

Benjamin sniffed in annoyance. "He was ten years old then."

Mr. Aaron looked at me. "I hadn't thought of that." After a moment he said, "Why didn't we meet his parents?"

"How do I know?" said Benjamin, acting more irritated

than he was. "Maybe he didn't come with his parents.
Maybe he's an orphan. Anyway, you can ask him this
afternoon."

This was news. "He's coming?"

"From Singapore," said Benjamin. He had withheld
the information, the old person's privilege and pleasure.
"I just got a cable. His people in Hong Kong must have
rung him up there—his bank has a Singapore branch. I
don't know the details. He's due in at two-twenty."

"I hope the plane's on time," said Mr. Aaron. "The
burial's at three. We can hold it up for a little while. But
if he's late?"

"Who's picking him up?" I asked.

"Morris," said Benjamin. Morris is the Honorary Aus-
trian Consul in Surabaya, and with the CC plates on his
car he can be counted on to get through the airport con-
fusion with the least delay.

"I hope the plane's on time," said Mr. Aaron again.
He looked out the window. "I would go over to my house
if it weren't for those women. Their weeping upsets me
worse than Abe's coffin. Would it be disrespectful to have
a drink? It's a hot day."

Benjamin got a bottle of whiskey, three glasses and a
bucket of ice. We drank without speaking, in the still,
dusty air of the narrow parlor, sitting in hard chairs. I
propped myself up on a cushion and tried to think of
something to say. One disadvantage about drinking in
silence is that you become self-conscious if you drink
quickly. I sipped mine. Benjamin held his drink under his
nose and inhaled it.

We had walked to Benjamin's, followed by *betjak* drivers, a half a dozen of them cycling along urging us to ride.
Mr. Aaron told them we weren't going far. It didn't do
any good. Now the *betjak* drivers—I could see them
through the barred windows of Benjamin's parlor—were
curled in the seats of their green vehicles, their feet resting
on the handlebars, parked in front of the house. Their
number had attracted a few hawkers, some women selling
fruit and one man with a noodle stall on wheels. "Have
some respect for the dead," I was going to say to them.
I thought: In a few hours Sassoon will be in the ground
and I can go home and sleep. I was sorry it was Saturday;

that meant a whole day tomorrow with nothing to do
except think about him. I'd rather go to work after a
funeral, to remind myself that I can still work.

Someone out front sat up in his *betjak* and began shouting. His hat was still pulled down over his eyes. They're
always camped against your fence. Mr. Aaron said,
"Lool's right. It is awful."

Lool's crazy, I was going to say: Why should death
make someone your brother? But that truth was an in-
appropriate argument.

Ponderously, Benjamin addressed his glass: "Sassoon
was a good man. He had some money, but he was a very
simple man—" He went on, and Mr. Aaron agreed. I
knew what was starting and I dredged around for a com-
plimentary reminiscence of old Sassoon.

The word that came to me was: *ruins*. We had seen
them at Sassoon's house in Tretes. I said, "Look at that,"
but Mr. Aaron had gone straight into the house. I was
standing under a mango tree—fruit had ripened and
dropped and turned black on the ground—and I was looking toward the back of the house. Once it had belonged
to a Dutchman, a happy one to judge from the back gar-
den. There was a swimming pool, children's swings, a
miniature golf course with toy bridges and stone chutes
and plump low posts. The swimming pool was sooty, filled
with tall weeds; the bolts of the diving board remained,
but they were large with rust. The swings were rusty, too,
the chains had snapped, and the odd stone shapes of the
golf course, sticking up from the overgrown yard, looked
like the baffling gravestones you see in a Chinese burying
ground.

It was dusk, soon dark as a cellar, and I wasn't sure I
had seen all those decaying, neglected things: I couldn't
verify in the blackness what might have been my imagination. I went into the house. Later, Mr. Aaron said the
house held the smell of death, but what I noticed was an
odor of vinegar and cabbage, boiled meat—probably what
Abe had eaten the previous evening. That, and the man-
goes which, newly rotting on the ground, gave off a high
ripe smell and filled the house with sweetness.

"We should be starting," Mr. Aaron was saying in
Benjamin's parlor.

I had been daydreaming. On the way I told them a story the cook had told me about Abe's giving the Javanese kids English lessons at night.

"And look what he gets for it," said Benjamin.

The signboard, lettered *Graveyard for Foreigners* in yellow and blue—but in Indonesian—was nailed to a high archway at the entrance. There was a little argument at the parking lot over our taking the van in. A Javanese came out carrying a long, rusty *parang;* he laughed when he saw us glancing at his knife, and he explained that he was head gardener. We'd have to leave the van outside, he said, and carry the coffin ourselves. Benjamin told him to lower his voice. We had attracted ten to fifteen onlookers, young boys mostly, in faded shirts. They watched us, smiling, as we heaved the coffin onto our shoulders and shuffled up the dusty road.

Benjamin walked in front, with his head down. Mr. Aaron and I were at the head of the coffin, Solomon and Lang had the other end; and behind us walked Mrs. Aaron, Benjamin's daughter and her husband—the Manassehs—Mrs. Lang, Mrs. Solomon and Joel Solomon. Joel is a fleshy fifteen-year-old with a big backside and mustache fur on his upper lip. We must have looked very strange, walking so solemnly in our black clothes, past the torn and carved-up trunks of the casuarina trees which lined the road, their needles glistering in the bright sun and making a mewing moan, a sinuslike sound over our heads—an especially odd sound, for the breeze causing it didn't drift near the hot road, and we could hear the coolness we couldn't feel. Squatting around these trees and next to scarred sisal clumps were groups of boys, most of them about Joel Solomon's age, captivated by the sight of eleven black crows marching with a box through the heat.

At the top of the road we turned right, past a monument in white marble with black graffiti painted on the wide plinth. There had been names and dates carved into the peeling casuarinas, and more names—nicknames, names of gangs—were painted on the gravestones. But it didn't strike me as blasphemous to scrawl your name on a broken monument or carve it into a dying tree. Down the cinder path, on an embankment, two goats were ripping grass with their lips, brushing the ground with their beards, their hoofs planted on *Rudy van Houten Feb. 1936–Dec. 1936*, a tombstone not much bigger than a water-swollen bread loaf: *Rust zacht kleine lieveling en tot wederziens*. A little farther along there was a broken, lamed angel, face down in the grass. There were no trees anywhere—we had left the moaning casuarinas behind— and the ground was so dry it opened in jagged cracks the width of your heel, big enough to trip you. The cloudless sky was enormous without the trees, and the flat plain of graves, the markers leaning this way and that, pushed over by the eruption of a rough grassy tussock—not even green—and scarred and scratched with charcoal—this baking plain was the kind you sometimes see in remoter places in east Java, a few acres of stony rubble signifying a dead story of habitation, which people visit to photograph. But this was not very far gone—more like Sassoon's own swimming pool, blackened and filled with tall grass, a recent ruin, in an early, unremarkable stage of decay, obviously crumbling but not far enough for alarm or interest. I wanted this history to be dust, and the dust to blow away.

We passed the children's graves. The next were families—stone shelters, flat white roofs on posts. Three boys sat under one for the shade, playing cards and listening to loud music on a portable radio. They looked up as we passed, and I heard Solomon curse them. I was fascinated by the heated ruins, the grasshopper whine, the awful litter inspiring not funereal sadness but the simple familiarity of this as a dumping ground in an old country with so many junkyards of cracked tombs and smashed statuary anyone can cart away. Here was a cluster of Chinese graves, photographs of old men and old black-haired women, wincing in eggsized lockets and posed like the faces in newspapers of men wanted by the police, but much more blurred: *Anton Tjiung Koeng Li*, and beside those stacked slabs, another set of slabs with deep, once gold letters: *Hier Rust onze Dierbare echtgenoot em vader Hubertus Tshaw Khoer Tan*. I had never been a pallbearer here, and today the slow march down the cemetery path, the fact that I was carrying a heavy coffin on my shoulder, made me curious about the details of the graves I was passing: *Geboren Solo 1877*, *Batavia 1912*, *Pontianak 1883*, *Soerabaja 1871*. The Dutchman born in Solo died in Surabaya. I saw a husband and wife; both were born in Malang, both died there: what journey? The next stone made me pause, and the coffin lurched as I read it: *In Memoriam Augusta Baronesse van Lawick-Hercules*. I made a point of remembering it for Mr. Aaron.

The Jewish corner of the cemetery adjoins the Chinese Buddhist section on one side, with a dingy crematorium the size and shape of a warehouse on the other side. I was hoping our section would be either in good repair or completely fallen to bits and covered by ashes and gnawed at and pissed on by goats. It was neither; in that intermediate stage of decay that characterized the whole place, a crack through a name, a date effaced, a dry turd cake against a column, weeds uncut, it was resisting pathetically, in the squeezed posture of indignity—but you knew it would disappear. Small boys with grass clippers and sickles had been following us, hoping for a chance to earn a few rupiahs trimming the weeds on our plot. As soon as we arrived at our corner, Mrs. Solomon and Mrs. Aaron turned and hissed to shoo them away. The boys stepped back, but this wasn't good enough: the women didn't want these urchins to watch. Mrs. Solomon pretended to chase them. The boys ran, stopping once to see if she was still after them.

We had put the coffin over the narrow, newly dug trench, and I was wiping my face. Benjamin compared his watch with Mr. Aaron's. "I thought he might catch up with us. I don't see any sign of him." Benjamin shaded his eyes and looked down the path.

"Let's give him ten minutes or so," said Mr. Solomon.

"The sun," I said, wrinkling my nose and squinting. "We should move over there." I felt a whiskey headache creeping across the back of my eyes. Our black clothes weren't doing us any good. "Mrs. Aaron," I said. "Wouldn't you like to stand over there, in the shade?"

"I won't leave him," she said, nodding at the coffin.

"Irma?"

"No."

Mrs. Aaron shook out her umbrella and pushed it open.

"Very nice," I mumbled to Mr. Aaron, "we all get sunstroke." Just behind him I read: *Mÿn geliefde broer Hayeem Mordecai Mizrahie.*

I closed my eyes and imagined myself keeling over; I was on my feet when I opened them, and the sun's dazzle blinded me. I held the lapels of my jacket and worked them back and forth trying to fan myself. Sweat crawled down my chest like harmless ants, tickling the hairs there, and my eyes were stinging with salt. I read the grave-markers to pass the time; it might have looked like veneration. *Our beloved Hilda Wife of Adolf Lisser Died 19th Elool 5701—11th Sept. 1941,* and a little lozenge-shaped stone, *Joseph Haim Bar 4½ Years.* I counted the ones born in Baghdad: two, three, five—six altogether, one with the inscription *Born in Baghdad (Aged 49) Died on Wed. 28th Nov. 1945.* That was Issac Abraham, but something was missing on his stone: where had he died, a Wednesday in what place? It was Tjimahi, the concentration camp in west Java—I knew him there. It would be forgotten. Here was a mispelled one: *These memory of loving uncle Solomon Judah Katar—Decierd* (what was that?) *10 Feb. 1945 Saterday Tjimahi Kamp His Soul Rest in Peace.* Not quite rubble, not yet incomprehensible: I wanted them dust, or else impossible to decipher, nameless as the stone with the top half missing and only *Died on Sat. Night 13 June 1926.*

"We should start," said Mr. Lang. Thank God, I thought.

"Do you hear a car?" asked Benjamin. He nibbled air, listening.

"It's those trees down there," said Mr. Aaron.

I read: *Selma Liebman-Herzberger.*

"Maybe Morris got a puncture," said Mr. Solomon.

"I'm thinking of the women," Mr. Lang said. "If it was just me I'd wait until five, or even later. But these women can't take the heat. Look. Covered with sweat, your wife's back. I'd hate to see one of them faint. Something like that would hold things up."

"Lool was awake most of the night," said Mr. Aaron.

"That's what I mean," said Mr. Lang.

"So was my Irma," said Mr. Solomon. "Her feet are

killing her." He looked in her direction. "She never complains."

"Look at this," I said, holding my jacket open. My shirt was darkly plastered, bubbled in places, on my chest. "Sopping wet!"

"I didn't think it would take so long for Morris to get here from the airport," said Benjamin.

"It shouldn't," said Mr. Lang. "That's why I suggested we start."

"If David thinks so—" I started to say.

Benjamin was looking uneasy. He didn't want to make the decision alone. He said, "Who thinks we should go ahead?"

"I do," said Mr. Lang promptly.

"Who's this cousin?" Mr. Solomon was asking Mr. Aaron.

"I'll go along with David," I said.

Mr. Solomon and Mr. Aaron nodded, and "All right, then," said Benjamin. The women were still standing around the coffin, holding their shiny black handbags tightly against their stomachs. Mrs. Aaron was sharing her umbrella with the Manasseh girl. Benjamin said, "We've decided to start."

"What about Glassman?" asked Mrs. Aaron.

"He's not coming."

The coffin rested on two beams which had been placed across the trench of the grave. Benjamin stood on the red mound of dirt lumps that had been shoveled out. We made a little circle around the coffin and listened to Benjamin read the prayers. The cover of his leather-bound siddur had sweatstains on it from being carried in the heat, black finger marks on the cover, a black patch on the spine.

He started reading slowly, but after a few verses his voice quickened to a reciting pace, a hurrying drone that emphasized only the last word before he sucked in a breath. The death chant for Abe Sassoon was being muttered to himself; this speeded rendition made it private. *Jakob Sassoon*, I was reading on the stone next to Benjamin, *Born in Baghdad*, and then Joel Solomon's whining voice, "Dad, I hear a car."

It was the screech of a car braking in gravel, and one after another, two doors slamming. We all heard.

Benjamin slowed down and read in a louder voice. Each of us sneaked a look down the dusty path to the entrance, but only the little boys were on the path. Two figures in black appeared, both running—one on long legs was far ahead of the other. This was Glassman, for just as I had turned to concentrate on what Benjamin was saying, he was on us. He came panting, a yarmulke in his hand, his face red, preparing to frown. We made room for him, and he fell on his knees beside the coffin, at the same time clapping the yarmulke on his head. He let out a great affronted wail. The women stopped crying and stared at him. Benjamin faltered in the verses, then continued, as Glassman hugged the coffin, knocking our black-bowed wreath askew. Now Glassman was crying piteously.

Benjamin stopped reading.

"Why stop now?" said Glassman angrily to Benjamin, a youthful quaver in his voice. "You started without me— *why stop now!* Go ahead, if you're in such a hurry!"

Benjamin lifted the book and read slowly.

Mrs. Aaron touched Glassman's shoulder. He raised himself, slapping the dust off his knees, to stand next to her. He had an expression on his face that showed horror and pain, his lips pressed shut, his cheeks blown out, his eyes narrowed to slits, his crumpled yarmulke slightly to one side.

I listened for Benjamin but I heard Glassman, who was breathing heavily, making a thin whistling in his nose and heaving his chest up and down and nodding his head with each long breath. He was wearing a beautiful suit. With the distraction of Glassman's panting, and with his screams still ringing in my ears, I felt a sharp embarrassment that was becoming terror.

It was time to put the coffin into the grave. We lifted the ropes under each end while the beams were slid away. Glassman watched us. We lowered the coffin on the ropes and Benjamin scooped up some dirt with a spade and threw it in, and said a prayer after it. Each person took a turn with the spade, the first ones making very loud thuds with their dry dirt clods on the coffin lid, the later ones making no sound at all. Glassman, the last to throw in some dirt, burst into fresh tears as he did so. He peered down. I have heard of close relations leaping into the grave, and I was afraid that Glassman might try this, perhaps breaking his leg. He shook his head—but he was indignant rather than sorrowful. What did he expect? Javanese *babus* in shiny silk pajamas holding umbrellas over our heads, a gilded coffin, the hot air split by mourners' shrieks, a wise old rabbi chanting into his nest of beard, a resolute throng of relatives at the graveside, shaking their fists at death? I knew this Glassman: "Why not try Manila or Hong Kong?" He walked back to where he had been standing, under Mrs. Aaron's umbrella.

"Brothers and sisters," said Benjamin. He spoke in Dutch, tasting each syllable separately, relishing the long words and closing his eyes as he finished a phrase. "These are very sad days for us—"

"What's that?" Glassman's shout made me jump. "What are you saying?"

We looked at him, then at Benjamin.

Benjamin proceeded, "But we must remember that our brother Abraham is now in a happy—"

"Stop that!" screamed Glassman, his voice cracking.

Benjamin glanced into the partially filled grave. He looked up and bit on a word which, displaying his teeth, he showed Glassman on the tip of his tongue. "Home," he said in Dutch, "he is home now. And someday—"

"What the *hell* is going on here?" Glassman asked Mrs. Aaron. "This is a bloody mockery. I won't have him talking in that language."

"Ben," said Morris. "Maybe you should—"

"And someday," Benjamin continued, more rapidly, "we will join our brother. Joyfully, yes, our hearts full—"

"No!" Glassman broke away from Mrs. Aaron, who reached for him. He vaulted the grave and his hands were on Benjamin's throat. Mr. Lang snatched at Glassman's arms, I yanked on his collar; it took five of us to pull him away. He kicked out, catching me on the shin with the sharp heel of his fancy buckled boot. "You!" he shouted at Benjamin. "What are you saying?"

Benjamin clasped his hands and tried to finish: "We should not mourn our brother—we should be glad he is at peace—"

"Let me *go!*" yelled Glassman, struggling.

"—enjoying the rewards of a virtuous life and hard work and let us all say a silent prayer for him."

We released Glassman and bowed our heads, praying silently. Glassman was surprised at his sudden freedom and then enraged by our silence. A yellow and gray bird with a head like the top of a claw hammer flew past.

"Shame on you," said Glassman while we prayed. "You should be ashamed of yourselves. What kind of people are you?" He went on in this vein, in his British accent, accusing us of savagery, looking quite comical with his jacket twisted around and his yarmulke slipping off and the knot of his tie pulled down and made small.

Benjamin signaled to some workmen to fill the hole. These three men in faded clothes had been standing under the eaves of the crematorium and had seen the whole business. They smiled as they ambled out of the shade, squinting and ducking as they entered the bright sunlight, and holding their spades ready.

Glassman, leaning, held each woman's shoulders and kissed her cheek. He left with Morris.

"What does it matter?" Benjamin said, when we were in the car and driving back to town. "It's his own fault for being late. *Bleddy mockery*." He snorted. "I wonder what they do in Hong Kong."

"The next problem," Mr. Aaron said—he hadn't been listening to Benjamin—"is where does he stay?"

It wasn't a problem. Glassman was on the evening flight to Djakarta. The rest of us stayed just where we were, and no one said that young man's name again.

horse his ... ... hair and more feeble than she now
been in the